Papi

ALSO BY RITA INDIANA

Ruminantes (1998)
La estrategia de Chochueca (1999)
Ciencia succión (2002)
Nombres y animals (2014)

Papi

RITA INDIANA

Translated by Achy Obejas

THE UNIVERSITY OF CHICAGO PRESS

Chicago and London

RITA INDIANA—also known as La Montra, the monster, in her role as the lead singer of Rita Indiana y los Misterios—is a pop artist, queer activist, and rising star of contemporary Caribbean literature. She is the author of two short story collections and three novels. Born in Santo Domingo, she lives in Puerto Rico. ACHY OBEJAS is a Cuban American journalist, writer, and translator. She lives in Oakland, CA, and Chicago.

The University of Chicago Press, Chicago 60637
The University of Chicago Press, Ltd., London
Papi © 2005, 2011 by Rita Indiana
English translation © 2016 by The University of Chicago
All rights reserved. Published 2016.
Printed in the United States of America

25 24 23 22 21 20 19 18 17 16   1 2 3 4 5

ISBN-13: 978-0-226-24489-1 (paper)
ISBN-13: 978-0-226-24492-1 (e-book)

DOI: 10.7208/chicago/9780226244921.001.0001

Library of Congress Cataloging-in-Publication Data
Hernández, Rita Indiana, 1977– author.
    [Papi. English]
    Papi / Rita Indiana ; translated by Achy Obejas.
        pages ; cm
    Summary: Papi tells a story in the voice of an eight year old girl waiting in Santo Domingo for her father to return from New York to lavish her with gifts and the glory of his fame. Things don't go according to plan.
    ISBN 978-0-226-24489-1 (pbk. : alk. paper) — ISBN 978-0-226-24492-1 (ebook)
    I. Obejas, Achy, 1956– translator.   II. Title.
    PQ7409.2.H355P3613 2016
    863'.7—dc23

♾ This paper meets the requirements of ANSI/NISO Z39.48-1992 (Permanence of Paper).

MICHAEL: "You know, you're about as much fun as a divorce . . . which is not a bad idea."

KITT: "I want custody of me."

—*Knight Rider*

one

Papi is like Jason, the guy from *Friday the 13th*. Or like Freddy Krueger. But more like Jason than Freddy Krueger. He shows up when you least expect him. Sometimes when I hear that scary music, I get really happy cuz I know he might be coming this way. That scary music is sometimes just Mami telling me Papi called and said he's picking me up to take me to the beach or shopping. I pretend I don't care, like I'm sure he's not coming cuz you don't get told ahead of time if you're about to get your head slashed by a machete; that's why those dummies go straight up to the bushes or the closet, where there's a mysterious light spilling out, and say, Helen? Or better yet: David? Even though everybody knows it's not Helen or David behind the bushes but Papi, raising his aluminum softball bat or an ax or a pick.

Papi's there, around any corner. But you can't sit down and wait for him cuz that's a longer and more painful death. It's better to make other plans, to just stay in your PJs and watch cartoons from six in the morning until midnight, or even go out for a stroll, which is a game

Mami made up for herself called if-Papi-wants-you-he-can-come-find-you. But Jason knows better than that and he disappears for months and even years, until I forget he exists, and then the scary music turns into Papi himself honking his car horn, and I go down the stairs four at a time so he can make mincemeat out of me just as soon as possible.

But what makes Papi most like Jason isn't that he shows up when you least expect him but that he always comes back. Even when they kill him off. When Papi left for the United States the first time with some Cuban woman who didn't want him sending anybody money, my abuela Cilí said, He's dead to me. And when Papi told Mami he was gonna get married again but not to her, she said, As far as I'm concerned, you're dead. And I think one time, when Papi stood me up, I called him on the phone and told him, I hope you die. I imagine there are so many other people who wanted him dead, like Jason, that it wouldn't take a detective to figure out that when it was our turn with the knife, we stuck it in not just once but a bunch of times (and since there were so many of us, and it was so dark, who was gonna count?). Anyway, nobody ever goes to jail for killing Jason.

That's why when they told me he was coming back, I'd already stopped waiting for him a long time ago and had imagined his return a million times: the clothes Papi would wear, how he'd step off the plane sniffing at the salty air, kneeling to kiss the ground.

And then, I'd already pictured this too: how he wears Nike running shoes and a two-thousand-dollar suit, and while the immigration official asks if he's just visiting, Papi gets in a runner's position—his hands on the ground, one leg straight back and the other bent beneath him—

and when the stamp falls on his passport, he goes off like a gunshot, running and running and his mind runs too, from Las Américas International Airport to La Feria, to the front of the Lotería Nacional building, to his mother's house, just like he'd promised Gregorio Hernández (the witch doctor), if only he'd grant him his wish to be rich, and now he's back and all that money he's been saving has come back with him.

We've been saving up for him, too; we've been waiting for you, Papi.

I'm waiting for you on the balcony at your mother's house, at Cilí's. I'm waiting for you with clenched fists and my mouth up against the balcony's cold railing, imagining how you're gonna leap from the car to the balcony (which is on the third floor) and how you're gonna hoist me up and say I'm so much bigger now you can hardly carry me, but of course, you're always gonna be able to carry me and so you lift me up and squeeze me and kiss my forehead, and I bury my head in your neck so I can smell your cologne from "over there," to see if you've changed colognes, just to see.

Everybody already knows you're back, that you're coming back, that you're coming home in triumph, a big shot with more gold chains and more cars than the devil himself. Everybody already knows. They're already imagining how you're coming back to them, to every single one of them, and how each one has been waiting for you, fantasizing about it, and telling the whole house, anyone who calls on the phone, the whole neighborhood: He's back.

They dream you fill your suitcase with gifts for them, that you work only for them, live only for them; in their dreams you owe them everything. They imagine your reunion. You, in your silver suit, your jet-black shoes, running from the airport or—even better!—paying for a plane to fly you from the airport to their houses, first of all, to knock on their doors and shower them with green bills that taste like confectioners' sugar.

The day comes and all of them, each and every one, awaken, drench themselves with a bucket of water, and take a good look at themselves. Today is the day, the day when they will know what's good, the day when you'll repay them for all they gave you when you were just a street kid—all those matches they let you borrow, the beer dregs they offered you, the ball bearings from the car engine they let you have. A few have a mental list of each thing you owe them, and in their heads they write down what you're gonna bring them, the thing they think will best repay them. And when the list gets too long (cuz they've jotted down even the times they said hello to you), they start to borrow, to go into debt, to squander that fortune they already feel is theirs, that fortune that will inevitably illustrate the perfect trajectory of a radiant shitstorm from your pockets to their faces, their hands, their mouths, all over their chests: your nieces and nephews, cousins, siblings, friends, your siblings' siblings-in-law, your nearest and dearest, neighbors, classmates, aunts and uncles, godparents, compatriots, the friends of that guy who's married to the lady whose brother is some dude who graduated from the navy a year after you.

Now they're organizing, gathering on both sides of the palm-lined avenue cuz they've all had the same idea of going to meet you. They're prepared, with placards in their hands, flags, little signs, banners that say, Güelcon Güelcon! The ones who weren't so quick now climb the palm trees on Avenida Las Américas and pluck them bare so they can lay the green fronds at your feet; others lay their own bodies down on the asphalt so you can walk over them; still others come with trucks wired with speaker towers blasting José José's "El Triste" cuz one night when they offered you some picapollo, that song was playing and they think it might be a good way to refresh your memory. Still others come in pickups with tinted windows, loudspeakers on the roof proclaiming slogans and stories about them and you. Others come disguised as members of the Civil Defense so they can shove people around and say, Let's move along, let's move along, waving batons and wearing those little orange vests that you can tell are homemade from a mile away. Then the people finally get organized and sign their names in a book some lady is passing around (she also sells peanut brittle) so you can see who came to welcome you and who didn't. The plane can be seen descending and women start to go into a trance and froth at the mouth while the men, legs trembling post-orgasm, dance "El Perrito" while holding on to the car bumpers.

Then here you are, here you are running over. People have lined up on both sides of the avenue; a rope keeps them away from your body but they stretch their arms so you can high-five them without slowing down. You've already doffed that two-thousand-dollar suit and are now wearing a seventeen-hundred-dollar, cobalt-blue jogging ensemble. It's starting to rain and people pull out umbrellas and plastic to cover themselves. Some lackey is just steps behind you with a piece of cardboard so your head won't get wet, but you're sweating so much it looks like you got soaked anyway. Behind you there's a caravan of cars with sirens, semis, trucks, motorcycles, and scooters, people running and others in wheelchairs and on bikes, keeping you in the spotlight with halogen lights while it rains cuz it's getting dark.

People begin to make out the caravan of driverless Pontiac Trans Ams, replicas Papi brought back to sell. Dozens of five-thousand-dollar suits brought back for Papi to wear. Thousands of watches, chains, white-gold rings and necklaces that adjust to Papi's body with a mere thought and that he thinks he'll wear to the grave. Somebody comes up with a baby in his arms so Papi can baptize him (the priest, the mother, and the altar boy with the baptismal font are running alongside him), and somebody kills a pig in Papi's name so a woman can catch up to him and bring a fork to Papi's mouth and he can blow on that roast pork and then, yum, eat it all up without missing a step. And so they slaughter chickens, goats, and guinea fowl all along the way, and running the whole time, Papi takes bites of everything. When a ragged parakeet, who's also running, sings "Compadre Pedro Juan" so he'll feel at home, Papi makes like he's dancing, with a hand on his belly and another in the air, wiggling his butt, all the while picking up the pace.

But before I can touch him, we see him on TV, slapping high fives from the airport to La Feria, trotting along, turning, trotting, sweating, running. Sometimes, and for just a couple of seconds, he walks and puts two fingers to his neck and looks down at his watch. Every two kilometers, two Civil Defense lackeys hand him a pair of blue Nikes, cuz his soles are wearing out, and the anchor on the six o'clock news—with a photo of Papi over his right shoulder—says, Quisqueya's darling son has returned, and they replay the images they shot just minutes before: Papi baptizing a baby, an old woman sticking a piece of pork in his mouth, Papi smiling and holding his hands together above his head like a winner. The screen also shows the cars and chains and an overwhelmed pregnant woman swooning.

I go out to the balcony to see if he's here yet, but all I see are the TV station's vans waiting for him, a line of newscasters on the sidewalk, mics in hand, pointing up here. I wave at them from Cilí's balcony, and when I go back inside to see if the news can tell us where Papi is, I see myself on the screen, waving from Cilí's balcony.

two

My Papi has more of everything than your papi, he's stronger than yours, he has more hair, more muscle, more money, and more girlfriends than yours. My Papi has more cars than yours, more cars than the devil, so many cars he has to sell some cuz they don't fit under his carport. Papi has cars that talk and tell you to put on your seat belt and shut your mouth in English, French, and other languages. Papi drives a different one each day, cuz there are so many he has to divvy them up, one for the morning, one for the afternoon, and another for the evening, that is, every four hours. Sometimes even a different one at lunch. One to pick me up at school, one for my First Communion, one to visit me on Sundays, one to visit his mother and another to visit his sisters, a Jaguar for Father's Day, a Camaro for Valentine's, a Bee Em Double U for grand openings, a Ferrari to take me for ice cream—a different one every four hours. There's one car he uses to bring Mami child support, one for when he comes to tell Mami he wants to get back with her, and another (usually a little Mercedes convertible) when he comes to tell us he's gonna marry another woman and invite us to the wedding and leaves Mami's furniture reeking of his cologne, which is strong, very strong, stronger and more expensive and better than the cologne used by your papi, if in fact your papi has ever even laid eyes on such a thing.

It all gives Mami a headache.

Papi has cars with black windows that filter out even the thinnest ray, and he has little black curtains for them to make sure not even the slightest light can get in. Cars that tell you who left the door open and who's eating their boogers, long fat cars, cars with doors that lift open, that make people gather around before we've even gotten out, that make a bunch of kids and teens and old people— almost all of them black and barefoot—come running to touch them cuz they think Papi and I have landed in a spaceship, almost always right in front of a beer hall or car wash on the Malecón, and they come to touch us and the car and they ask Papi about the car, about me and the car, and Papi answers without looking their way, as if it weren't important, as if cars have always flown, as if Papi and I touch down every afternoon in a car that seems like a spaceship in front of all the beer halls on the Malecón, which is in fact true.

Papi gets out of the car and leaves the door open so kids, young and old (almost all black and thin and barefoot), can climb in and turn on the wipers and the lights and open the doors that flip up like the wings of a seagull, like a spaceship. Sometimes Papi even gives them the key so they can turn it on and fly off, but they're so stupid they circle around about three times and then crash into the sea or the reef off the Malecón, or they get tangled in the electrical wires like a pair of dead shoes.

Papi doesn't care. Not if they kill themselves or if they

9

leave the cars impaled on top of a coconut tree, since he has so many. What Papi does is whip out a camera and take a Polaroid photo of the accident so he can give it to the surviving kids, teens, and seniors; as soon as we turn our backs, they beat the heck out of each other for that photo.

My Papi has so many clothes and so many closets to keep them in that sometimes, when he wants to wear a particular shirt, he has to buy it new cuz he forgets which closet he put it in. And he has so many Polo shirts, with that little guy playing polo on his chest, that he has about fifteen closets just to keep the Polo shirts; if he wanted, one shirt for each day of his life. All those Polo shirts, even after they're washed, still smell all the time of Papi's cologne; even after they're washed, it clings to them, and even though Papi sends them out to get cleaned, it won't go away so that when Papi changes cologne he has to change all his clothes too and buy them all new and start again.

My Papi has more cars than the devil. My Papi has so many cars, so many pianos, so many boats, submachine guns, boots, jackets, overcoats, heliports, my Papi has so many boots, and then more boots, my Papi has so many girlfriends, my Papi has so many boots, cowboy boots with eagles and snakes etched into the leather, leather boots, rubber boots, black boots, brown ones, red ones, white ones, caramel colored, wine colored, olive green, blue like the blue on the flag. Ugly boots, too. Boots to play polo and cut the grass. Boots for off-roading. My Papi has motorcycles, scooters, ninja bikes, domestic animals, four-wheel drives, and velocipedes. Papi has curly hair, black and curly, cuz when he was a sailor and wore uniforms—white, khaki, boots, a wooden gun, a fake gun just for photos—my Papi's hair was very short, cuz in the wartime navy they shaved it off with an electric razor that went *zoom zoom* and cut what was left of his blond hair. Papi was very blond when he was little—his hair was practically white, almost albino, and very straight and very long—cuz one day he'd choked on a piece of plantain, and as he was turning black as an olive his mother promised the Virgin of Altagracia that if he were saved from the plantain, she'd let his hair grow long, which is why in all the photos Papi has very blond, very straight, very long, long hair. They took a lot of pictures but you could almost never see his face, just his very long hair, and when you could see his face, he looked like a girl with a very long and very white braid that went almost to his waist.

But now his hair is black and thick and short, a mini-Afro. Papi has friends who comb it; they come over to comb it, with blow-dryers and a little round cylindrical brush that makes a *kra kra* sound in Papi's hair, which is very black and very curly. Papi's friends, who comb his hair and shave him and cut his nails and paint them with a bright transparent polish, also do me: they wash my hair in the sink and dry it with a towel and blow-dry it and use a round cylindrical brush, even bigger than the one they use on Papi, cuz my hair is still kind of blond, and not as straight, and not as long, or as albino. Later they use these magic drops on both our hair and they tell us we're beautiful and very much the same, and I look at myself in the mirror with my almost-blond mane and it's true that I'm almost the same as Papi.

The blow-dryer is Papi's, as well as the brushes, and a friend of his comes to wash and comb and dry our hair and paint our nails all different colors—mine are painted pink, which later flakes off. Papi has nail-polish remover in a little drawer full of nail files and pumice stones and hydrating creams and cocoa oil and Johnson's oil. His friend sits me on her lap and takes care of my pink cuticles with a little cotton ball and then another cotton ball that falls on the floor and looks as if it's bloody.

Papi loses track of how many jackets he has, gifts from friends who own discos, who had the jackets made for him, watches and caps with his initials embroidered in gold so they can be given away at inaugurations and New Year's Eve parties that Papi attends with a new girlfriend, a new car, and a new pair of boots. They're newer than anything you or your papi would have, if you actually even know what it means to have such things. Jackets with or without logos, blue, jackets like the kind baseball players wear, phosphorescent jackets, huge, quilted— jackets in which I disappear the moment I put them on, but I put them on anyway and I don't care, I put them all on as soon as Papi leaves and I am left alone with everything in Papi's closet. I go in all his walk-in closets and try on all his jackets and they all look great on me. They're a little big, but that's very trendy right now, I think, and so I put on one of Papi's jackets and a pair of Papi's boots and I walk down the hall between the first and the last closet trying on different combinations, making the boots go *clack clack clack* cuz I love that sound and it makes me feel like a cowboy, as if I lived in another world.

When Papi sees me in his jackets he says he starts sweating just looking at me wearing them, but I don't understand. He says he gets so hot just looking at me wearing them. So I keep them on and Papi sweats, sweats, sweats, sweats, sweats, sweats a lot. He gets red and looks as if he's about to explode. He tells me these are winter jackets. But I don't understand. He says those jackets are for winter. But I leave them on and now I'm also wearing a pair of Papi's Ray-Bans, gold ones, cuz Papi has more glasses than anybody, about one hundred and twenty pairs. Papi is sitting and watching *Rocky III* and they are knocking Rocky's head off while I'm putting on another jacket and Papi is turning to water. He is totally melting on the couch, the remote control floats in the little puddle that was his hand, but there's also a kind of steam cuz sweat evaporates very quickly, and so the remote falls on the floor and I start to take off Papi's jackets, one by one very quickly, cuz I don't wanna be without my dad, but by the time I remove the last one, Papi is just a sweat stain on the couch and the credits are rolling over Rocky's face as he screams, his mouth twisted: Adrian!!!!!

But it's not Rocky who's screaming—I got confused—it's really Papi, who drinks so much and gets so bummed. Papi has many bottles filled with all kinds of things and he drinks with his friends, who bring more bottles while they play dominoes with a gold set they gave Papi as a present; it was probably a gift from another disco owner. The clatter of the golden dominoes gets confused with the collision of glasses and bottles and ice. The servant, one of them, sees the price on the bottle and asks Papi if it's true the bottle costs more than she earns. But now Papi vomits next to the bed, a green vomit, green green, and then yellow and then yellow yellow and then pink and then a very dark red. I don't like this. Honestly. Papi vomits more than me, and I get nauseous from the minute the smell hits me and I run to put bayrum on my head and on my neck and to put ice under my arms. I'm getting sick, getting really sick.

Papi is dying, I am dying, but luckily Papi has an ambulance, two ambulances, each with a chauffeur and they come to take us to the dog track and so Papi and I are just sitting there, in our wheelchairs, watching the dogs chase a wooden rabbit while a nurse–flight attendant holds our IVs and checks them and adjusts the lever so they'll increase the flow. My Papi and I have been betting on the red dog not winning all afternoon, but the red dog keeps winning, and it's a lot of fun. Later, since Papi has friends everywhere, they give us a backstage tour and this is where we see the kennels and bathrooms, where there are little puddles of blood cuz sometimes the dogs die after the races and you can see garbage bags where the dead dogs' legs stick out. Later the dog track veterinarian lets me give a shot to a buttless greyhound—what joins the leg to the hip is just a piece of skin and he pisses right there, so that's where I nail the needle, which goes smoothly into the greyhound and then a black man shoves him back in his little cage.

Now we're getting better. Color returns to our skin. The fever goes down. Papi even shaves, which always makes him feel better cuz when he shaves he looks twenty years younger. Practically a boy. He's so small, so young, I can even carry him on my back. We're watching *Rocky III* again cuz it looks like, along with *Dirty Dancing*, it's the only thing playing this summer. Later Papi falls asleep on the couch and I make like I'm asleep too, sometimes opening just one eye to look at the scene of the two of us very close together with our eyes closed. The light of the television makes Papi look even more beautiful and I turn up the volume all the way on the TV so we won't hear Papi's girlfriends screaming, so those wretches won't wake him up since they've recently taken to gathering in the parking lot calling and calling him as they walk in a circle with placards and photos of Papi. They call me and then form a human tower, nailing their heels in each other's shoulders in order to reach the top floor of the tower, where I am with Papi.

Here they come now: skinny and tall ones, really fat ones, women who are all butt, big-assed, dark ones and red-haired ones, snub-nosed and hawk-nosed, titonic, synthetic, some with their tits sticking right up, others with aerodynamic hair—idiots caught between the gravitational pull of the sun and the moon, a frozen and lacquered tsunami suffering from premenstrual syndrome. Here they come, with fake fingernails on their lashes, with eyes on their nails, with their guts like this (and when I say, Like this, I use my right index finger to point to the bicep on my left arm, in other words, the guts should measure about a foot and a half), on stilts and surgical needles, on laser beams instead of needles. They have their own ships, motorcycles, and scooters which Papi bought for them, and they all come together on stationary bicycles to eat me alive, to choke me with a spoon and leave me with a semicircle tattooed on the roof of my mouth, a semicircle that means they forced me to eat, that they worry about my health and my well-being, that they're all good stepmothers and Papi has chosen well, so I should love them and put up with them and understand them and suck at the milk that seeps from their tits, their little tits, their big tits, and call them Mami, Mamita, Mamasota. They come at me like crazy women, shrieking, laboring with false pregnancies, giving birth to stuffed animals, to latex babies that pee when you squeeze their little bellies.

Here they come again, wiping the lipstick off their teeth with napkins from the pizza place, with dirty rags, the same rags with which they punctured my eardrum while cleaning my ears, and now they're coming with more wipes to clean what's left cuz they never get tired of wiping me, of shoving rags and enemas up everywhere when Papi's not around, when Papi runs out of here in a car he keeps parked on the balcony. He takes off every time they show up, screaming, cursing, pulling their brittle hair out until it just falls out of their heads like ceramic breaking on the granite floor as if it were dust.

Now the girlfriends are coming in semitrucks decorated with red plastic flags, the red and yellow flags of a political party, then the yellow and purple flags of another party, banners and confetti and red streamers in sound trucks with three-hundred-thousand-watt speakers, campaigning for themselves, beating themselves on the stomach and chest so intensely that sometimes an intestine peeks out, or an eye. They're furious, demonic, beautiful, horrible nobodies. They hate me, hate, hate, hate me, cuz they have to love me, love me, love me.

They're catching up to us, I tell Papi, and he pulls a pistol out from under the seat and passes it over. Shoot, he says, as he ducks his head behind the wheel cuz they're firing on us, throwing rocks at us, grenades, ceramic wigs that shatter very close to our chassis, our car, which is spinning donuts at two hundred miles an hour on the Malecón. I stick an arm out and fire and fire and fire, and you can hear Papi's girlfriends screaming as they fall from the parade floats, fatally wounded, grabbing their chests. I keep firing with the guns Papi keeps handing me without even glancing at me as he ducks his head, steering with his knees; he uses his other hand to push my head down so they won't kill us, so the bazookas those bitches are shooting at us will go right past our heads.

The parade floats are decorated with papier-mâché and crepe paper (Taino idols, Columbus skulls, many María Montezes) that light on fire and the hags spit to put them out but the hags' saliva has a highly combustible pH that makes whole floats go up in flames. The fire reaches their pantyhose while I continue emptying Papi's guns and hitting whores left and right into the crowds out enjoying the parade on both sides of Avenida George Washington. They clap their hands every time a hollowed-out whore falls from a float. I wave at the crowds and they wave bye-bye with their hands while they grab the dead women so they can steal their necklaces and bracelets.

Papi starts to lift his head but instead of an M16 he hands me a lollipop, a blue lollipop that turns my tongue an almost-black blue. I see myself in the rearview mirror and think—and this is just as we're taking off (cuz there's finally enough room on the freeway so we can lift off)— that I want Papi to buy me a chow chow, but before I can even say, Chow, Papi's girlfriends have been transformed: the papier-mâché Taino idol from the float, which is practically ashes now, has seen them and smelled their blood, and Papi's girlfriends' blood has cried out, and a salty wind has lifted the Taino god's ashes and covered the ravaged corpses. The terrified mob runs and tears at their own clothes cuz the dead women are transforming, convulsing, hitting themselves in the belly so hard that two wings break out from their flesh, two ribbed bat wings, two Batgirl wings, two devil wings, and they soar like protopterodactyls, dragoniles, daughters of their own cursed mothers. Papi and I reach an altitude of seven hundred thousand feet, eight hundred thousand feet, when one of the bitches sinks her fangs into our tires. Shoot, goddammit, shoot, says Papi, who has forgotten to give me a gun, and I pull the lollipop from my mouth and I lean almost all the way out of the car window (all this is going on at seven hundred thousand or eight hundred thousand feet, but Papi grabs me by the belt so I won't fall) and I shove my lollipop into the demon woman's eye as she screams loudly and falls, dragging all the others, one by one, to the bottom of the sea, raising a crown of froth, very white and very beautiful, at least from way up here.

Papi and I keep going up and up and up and we can't even see the sea anymore. The temperature just keeps going down and down and down, and Papi starts to shiver and I shiver, so we bring our hands together, cupping our hands and blowing. Papi turns on the car heater, which fills the car with an imitation heat that, even at its best, allows the cold to sneak in. Everything's white outside and I ask Papi if this is snow, if we're finally gonna need winter clothes. He says no, these are just clouds.

For a long time, this is all we see, just white and more white, until a yellow light seeps through and drenches everything and there's music too, a current merengue hit that goes like this: White kite that plays and ignores / that you're already mine. Later we can see the mango-colored neon sign in which a beer bottle eternally pours a stream of froth that spells out Car Wash. Two dark women wearing mango-colored anoraks come skating through the clouds and help us open the doors of Papi's car because, like I said before, they open by lifting up, but now they're stuck cuz the white frost has gotten into the slits and frozen over. The two black women, who've known Papi all their lives, help us get into a couple of mango-colored anoraks with white fur hoods. The anoraks (This car wash is first class, says Papi) have our names printed in silver. They're very pretty, and I'm delighted as we go into the car wash looking for a place among the rest of the clientele, who are dressed for the cold. Everyone's at the bar, leaning on little Formica tables. All the men have their hair cut the same way: a bun on top that they pull at with their index fingers and thumbs to make it seem more voluminous, a greasy little mane in back and designs on both sides—sculpted with both scissors and razor—featuring Sergio Valente's bull, stars of Bethlehem, or Tony Mota's face.

Through the picture window, you can see the clients' cars as the rest of Papi's ex-girlfriends—shackled at the neck by latex-covered chains that light up—squeeze huge sponges. Hoses spew foam that falls on their bodies the whole time, but these girls must be very cold cuz they're naked.

three

Then Papi goes shopping.

And I go with him.

Cuz he's my dad and I'm his daughter.

And Papi buys so many things, I forget how many. Papi has so much money, he has to carry a woman's purse; a man's bag is just not big enough. That's why he's always with a woman, so she can carry his purse. He has many purses, some that match his boots, most are leather and come in all sizes, very pretty and very refined. He also has many belts, some made of buffalo, rhinoceros, or Komodo dragon. That's why when we go shopping he brings along not just one but two or three women to carry his purses and his checkbooks and billfolds, so many billfolds that sometimes Papi prefers to just buy the whole store and stay there overnight among the air conditioners, freezers, blenders, TVs, and other domestic appliances.

When I was little, my dad used to carry me like a purse, or so he says: he used to carry me around just like a purse. And whenever he mentions this, I'm thrilled and imagine myself in a little seven-peso dress my mother bought me at La Sirena, a little dress I wear constantly, and Papi lifts me up and I'm riding on his side like a back-pack, like a package, a happy little purse, and Papi looks at me and tells me I wear that dress too much, and do I have other dresses or what. And do I have a dad or what, and do I have a mom or what. What's my favorite house, he asks, and that's when I think of Mami's house, with the two little rocking chairs, the poinsettia on the black-and-white TV set, and then later, after Papi's already put me down, we go to one of Papi's houses, of which there are, like, fifty. There are about seven cars parked at this one and there are always people delivering a new piece of furniture, a new stove, a new bottle with a crystal ship inside. Each house has a pool that Papi has personally filled with inflatable whales, dragons, inflatable Straw-berry Shortcakes, rowboats, motorboats (the pool is very big), miniature submarines Papi and I can crawl into and sometimes even one of his girlfriends too, who shouldn't even dream of looking out of the portholes, from which you can see all these monstrous sea creatures who live at the bottom of the pool and whom I bravely contemplate so Papi will notice me, so Papi will see I'm not afraid of anything.

Papi has prepped a room for me in each of his houses, and each one has its own dresser, its own nightstand, and its own accompanying little lamp, all made of white wicker. Each has its own bed and its own reversible quilt with Rainbow Brite on one side and Gremlins on the other. Papi has so many Rainbow Brites and Grem-lins that I can't stand them anymore. A whole closet full of Rainbow Brites and Gremlins. Papi's also bought me boots and Crayolas and alphabet stickers and pretested watercolors, Flexi-Foam sheets, Barbie wigs, sweat shirts,

Halloween decorations, wide-angle compact binoculars, rechargeable spotlights, a junior utility table, jerseys, gloves, leather gloves for winter for when I go visit him, for when Papi comes back and takes me with him.

Now he's got boneless skinless chicken breasts, whole boneless beef, mi nenes, Nintendos, try-on socks, tae kwon do classes, cashew nuts, semaphores, hotel-style turkey breast, boneless-beef shoulder roast, center-cut bone-in smoked ham steak, domesticated tarantulas in terrariums, Ledbetter boneless-beef bacon-wrapped tenderloin filets, Japanese lanterns made from Tibetan parchment paper, all-purpose white potatoes, women, all-purpose yellow onions, women, Campbell's tomato soup, chicken noodle, women, green bean–onion alphabet soup.

I have a throbbing pain in my knees cuz I'm growing too fast, which is why Papi sends me so many bikes, so that I'll take care of my knees. He sends me a bike a month, each bigger than the last, one for each leg, but what I need is one with training wheels cuz I'm afraid of falling, but we don't tell Papi so he just keeps sending them: red ones, yellow and green ones, just so rust will eat 'em up. This time he sends a cobalt-blue bike that has, like, seven speeds. But rust eats it up, they sell it off to another little girl, they give it away to a cousin, rust eats it up it, they give it away to the poor kids, they sell it, even if it has ET or Barbie mudguards.

Mami and I write a letter. Mami dictates and I write and Mami says my handwriting gets prettier all the time. In the letter we ask Papi for a color TV, we ask him not to send any more bicycles, that we want, that what I want, that what I need, is a color TV cuz the salt is eating up all those bikes.

But Papi writes back and says he's not gonna set up Mami's boyfriends to watch TV in color and so Mami and I write another letter in which I explain to Papi that I'm the one who wants the color TV, that Mami has nothing to do with it, that Mami doesn't have any boyfriends, that Mami just lives for me, and please, make it a Zenith, cuz they're the best, and Mami says my handwriting is really getting better.

Then Papi sends word that he's not gonna buy a TV for the good-for-nothings Mami keeps around. So we call on the phone and I tell Papi I wanna watch Bugs Bunny in color and he cries on the other end. I know this cuz he whimpers when he cries and then the doorbell rings and I open the door and there's Corporán de los Santos, the champion of Dominican TV, with his Afro, flanked by his seven Corporettes blowing confetti and streamers out their noses. He's come to deliver the TV Papi sent, and it comes in a box so big I can make a little house out of it as Mami and her boyfriend watch the seven-thirty telenovela.

I like TV a lot and I like playing a game I made up in which you point to things that come on the screen and say, Mine, so that the first person who says, Mine, is the owner of whatever that thing is. And since I'm almost always alone, I get to keep everything for myself, cuz I'm sure that wherever Papi is, he's already bought it all for me. Someday Papi will come back and things will be like before, better than before. We'll go shopping at dusk and get to the store just as it's about to close, and cuz we're in a big hurry cuz the clerks wanna leave, Papi will say, Just point to what you want with your finger, and then Papi tells whichever girlfriend he's brought along to get one in each color, and so we fill up carts with socks in every color, long ones and short ones, in every color, one in every style, with little pom-poms on the ankle. Later Papi drops me off at Mami's and she watches from the balcony as we unload everything from the trunk of the car. When night falls, I put on all my new socks, one on top of the other, and I make a corral on the bed with my new shoes. I lie down in the very center and try to sleep while breathing in that smell of newness, but I'm trembling from a fear of dying without having been able to try out all my new things.

And it's just that Papi has so much music you're always afraid he's gonna stop the song that's playing before it's over. He has a record player and a cassette player in each room and there's a record or a cassette ready to play in each one. Whenever people come over, Papi spends all his time running from one music machine to the other pressing Stop or Play or Rewind or Fast-Forward. Or Pause. Papi has a piece of furniture, actually a bunch, where he keeps his records; in fact, the walls are covered with shelves on which Papi's records gather dust and the servant—actually a whole bunch of servants—take care of them by dusting them off with a blue-velvet dust cloth.

There's a room full of merengue records in which the shelves reach the ceiling. And there's a room for American music and a little room for classical music, or as Papi says, dead people's music, and that room is really the bathroom.

Saturday mornings Papi gets up early and makes me breakfast himself so he has to run from the blender to the record player and from the stove to the toaster and from there to the cassette player. I get up wondering what all the racket's about. I walk slowly to the living room and spy Papi dancing, moving his little butt while wearing a red apron that says #1 Pimp, with Cuco Valoy's LP in one hand and a tray of waffles or mangú with fried cheese in the other.

Papi likes Cuco Valoy very much, though he's not one of my faves, especially when Cuco pulls out his little bell and says, And now we're gonna practice some brujería! I like Johnny Ventura and his Combo Show better, all of them wearing very tight pants. My tía Leysi says they all stick socks down their pants so they'll look bigger when they dance. They wear color-coordinated shirts unbuttoned down to their navels, leaving all that chest hair and all those gold chains out in the open. It's the same with Wilfrido Vargas. I think the chains send some kind of signal, like when you send messages from one rooftop to another with mirrors. Wilfrido plays the trumpet, which also reflects light, just like the trumpets and trombones and saxophones Conjunto Quisqueya and Fernandito Villalona play, except that when Fernandito's brass section plays they send signals that reflect Channel 9's spotlights, and then all the servants come down to suck up to Fernandito. The same thing happens with Bonny Cepeda and Los Kentons, except that Los Kentons wear karate uniforms, and they perform katas as they dance and kick the servants. But although Wilfrido kicks the mic stand, Cuco employs witchcraft, and Bonny's shiny hair-sprayed bun reflects back the light, nobody dances like Papi on Saturdays when we're alone and we practice in front of the wall-sized mirror in his apartment. He teaches me how to do a two-three, one-two-three-four, and dresses me up in his suits. We gel up our hair and use combs like mics and Papi drops the mic and runs to the record player or the phone and comes back so fast he's picked the comb back up before it even hits the floor and then he's teaching me another song.

Even more than the records, I like the record covers. The photos and drawings of the singers posing on wicker thrones or holding a mic as if it were a chicken leg. Black-and-white and color photos so you can see clearly who sings and who plays what. Some even include the lyrics to the merengues for those who can't figure them out by listening. Fernandito "El Mayimbe" wears a cowboy hat and sits on a rock, Cuco Valoy is beaten by a cop, and a kitten walks on Fausto Rey's shoulders, while Los Vecinos, with identical haircuts, stand around in white booties. Los Kenton are splitting up, Papi concludes as he stares at a record cover in which they join Bonny Cepeda for a concert with karate uniforms and Afros that grow smaller each year.

One day, on the *Show del Mediodía*, after they'd dragged Pololo off the set with a stroke, the news anchor appeared and looked up from some papers to say, We interrupt this program to inform you that Fernandito Villalona, alias "El Mayimbe," has been detained for possession of oregano and cilantro. The well-known interpreter of "La jamaquita" and "Tabaco y ron" was stopped near Calle 42 by a unit whose officers searched the glove compartment and found oregano and cilantro, as indicated by the tests used in these cases. Fernandito admitted in principle that the aromatic herbs found in the vehicle were his but now says the sale and use of same were actually his tía Bolivia's, who was making a sancocho in honor of her sister, the singer's mother.

There were voices coming from down the street, voices outside the TV: they got him with grass, they got him with grass. Returning to Studio A at Color Visión on Channel 9, Doña Zaida Lovatón, director of the Commission for Public Performances, whose gray streak looked exactly like

Cruella De Vil's, discussed the facts on live TV, rocking in a rocking chair from the comfort of her home: I said it once and I'll say it again, this poison has to be cut off at the roots . . .

Later, changing over to Channel 7, Julie Carlo (with a blond poodle perm), former star of the *Show del Mediodía* and now contracted to *Sabroshow*, covered her ear with two fingers cuz the brown mob was railing and pushing while waving El Mayimbe record covers in their hands. Before a lady hitting her own chest could grab the mic from her, Julie informed us: Fernandito Villalona was just set free. The attorney general of the republic has waived the charges against him. Repeat, El Mayimbe has been set free. And the mobs, which had taken to the streets in outrage cuz they'd locked up the spoiled star, jumped and shouted and El Mayimbe came out, handcuffs still on, next to that union guy José Francisco Peña Gómez, who showed off the silver key in his very black hand to the crowds and grinned with those teeth so white they reflected the scorching tropical sun as he released El Mayimbe, lifting his hands in the air like a boxer. All the while Peña hopped up and down, shaking them both. That's when Fernandito stepped back to get a running start and then launched himself from the top of the stairs into the multitudes waiting for him. We saw him floating above that black, red, blue, and white mob, and sometimes the only thing we could see were his Adidas and his flowered shirt and his little hat and his gold ring swimming above all that curly hair toward Rahintel's Studio B at Channel 7, where the recently launched *Sabroshow* was waiting for him. Wilfrido, Johnny, Bonny Cepeda, Rasputín, Cuco, Dioni Fernández, Belkis Concepción, Aramis Camilo, La Santini, Feli Cumbé, and Julie Carlo were also waiting for him. The orchestras and all the Channel 7 cameras were waiting with a contract that would free him from whatever responsibilities he had to any other variety show.

Fernandito, alias "El Mayimbe," who the crowd just dropped on the floor, signed and hugged Julie and, bringing his succulent white mulatto lips to the mic, began to tear up, and then I began to tear up, and then we all began to tear up. He said, Excuse me for coming here to sing like this, wearing tennis shoes, but I just got released from jail and I came right over so I didn't have time to change.

Then all the orchestras started playing (just think about how many trumpets, trombones, and saxes that means) the beginning of "Baila en la calle" at the same time, and Fernandito, just before he started singing, trying to get on top of the music, proclaimed: I dedicate this song to its composer, maestro Luis "Terror" Díaz.

Papi also has American music, and sometimes I'm the one who plays those records. I'm dancing the most complicated steps when the phone rings and Papi screams at me to turn it down down down and so I turn down the volume. When Papi hangs up, he orders me to turn it up up up and so I just dance with my hand glued to the volume control so I can turn it up or down when he tells me to.

Papi loves Billy Ocean.

One Saturday I get up and hear the beginning of "Caribbean Queen" by Billy Ocean but Papi is not making my breakfast. Instead, he's dropping a bunch of dead shrimp in boiling water, lobsters too. Thousands of 'em. And when I look through the door to the kitchen and see the overflowing stainless-steel pots, Papi says, That's so you'll taste some brain food. Papi also makes multicolored sauces and white rice and then he calls the corner store and tells them to deliver two bags of ice cuz his family is coming over today. I'm very happy my tía Leysi and my tía China and my abuela Cilí are coming over, and also my cousin Puchy and my cousin Milly, who are my father's other sister's kids, but she died in childbirth cuz they're twins and each weighed fourteen pounds.

My abuela Cilí raised the twins together with my tía Leysi and my tía China. Neither of them has ever married and they all live together in an apartment across the street from the Lotería Nacional. The apartment is on the third floor. Cilí bought it from Balaguer during his twelve-year presidency, after she sold her little plot of land and came to the city with her children and grandchildren, that is, the twins. Papi enlisted in the navy in order to eat shark meat, and Tía China enrolled at the Universidad Autónoma so she could hook up with black people and throw rocks. And although my tía Leysi is the same age as Milly and Puchy, when Cilí went to visit her people in the countryside, she left Leysi in charge. She took care of ironing their bell-bottomed pants and made sure they had matching orange polyester shirts and shiny strapless blouses. The three of them would then go to disco and salsa shows, sometimes even winning dance contests, money, fake jewelry, tickets to *Grease*. One day, Milly and Puchy won fifty pesos and used it to buy white fabric so they could each have a suit made exactly like John Travolta's on *Saturday Night Fever*. Almost always, they managed to find somebody who would take them home in a Cadillac at five o'clock the next morning. China was on her way back at that hour after putting up posters of Che Guevara all over Ciudad Nueva, though the police would tear them down before sunrise. The four of them would sit down at Junior's Chimichurri on the corner of the Lotería Nacional, where the sluts and the queens from La

Feria would offer each of them half a chimi and a 7 Up. They'd think about Papi (and when they thought about him, they imagined him in his sailor's suit giving them a military salute), and wondered whether Papi was on land or sea and if he'd been assigned a real rifle yet.

By the time Papi's family knocks on the door, the shrimp are ready. Papi knocks himself out trying to make them comfortable in the living room and showing them his new gadgets and taking each one aside so he can shove a roll of bills in his shirt pocket. Papi says, Go show Puchy and Milly your new toys, and I have them follow me, but as we walk down the hallway they take a detour into Papi's closets and begin to try everything on, even the cologne. I'm red with fury and tell them to leave that stuff alone, that it's Papi's, and they say Papi told them to take whatever they want, to take everything, so I foam at the mouth and kick but they don't care, stuffing jackets, pants, shoes, shirts, ties, and hats in a suitcase Papi gave them as well.

I throw a fit.

But what really burns me is that the twins are already sixteen and Papi can take them with him to his friends' discos. When they have plans, they start getting dressed very early, from the moment they wake up, laying out their clothes and accessories on the bed, dressing and undressing and looking at themselves in the mirror and suggesting things. Sometimes they even cut their hair like those guys from Tears for Fears in the video that goes, Shout shout shout it out loud. They stand in front of the TV with the scissors waiting for the video to come on. Milly puts on a black polka-dot shirt and uses a lot of mousse and Puchy colors a swatch of hair and adjusts the belt with the metal tip. Papi dusts them both off and Tía

Leysi—who's going too, cuz everyone but me is going—takes off her rollers and sprays her hair. Wait 'til you're big, wait 'til you're big, they tell me, cuz I've been pouting since I found out. They leave me with Cilí, who makes me sleep in her bed with my feet near her head so we both fit, but since I kick in my sleep she ties my heels to the headboard. I think, Damn, since Papi has so much money, you'd think Cilí would have a different lifestyle by now, at least a house with more beds and more TVs. When Cilí turns off the light and starts to whisper Psalm 23, her spit sprays in the dark and I imagine Papi, Tía Leysi, and the twins dancing with their cool clothes and their bracelets and their hairdos.

The party features Fernandito Villalona. And that makes me throw a bigger fit.

The next day, trying to get me to forgive him for not taking me, Papi lets me sit on his lap while he drives. I grab the wheel the whole time we're on a very long drive that always ends up at some girlfriend's of his, always with a bigger butt than the previous girlfriend, and with even more gold chains. On the way back I want a raspberry Country Club soda and Papi says, Let's see if they have change at this convenience store and the clerk shakes his head no; the problem is Papi only has thousand-peso bills. Papi just stands there with a roll of pink bills in his hands and I look at him and the clerk looks at me and I look at the bottle of raspberry Country Club on the shelf and Papi looks at his pink roll and the clerk looks at the roll and I look at the bottle of red soda and the pink bills and I think the bills and the Country Club match. I look at a box of straws and at the poster next to the store's door that says for every ten Country Club bottle caps of any color plus five pesos you can get a yo-yo. Then, in the silence that smells like Cubanelle peppers, the only audible sound is Papi's finger sliding down the edge of the roll of thousand peso bills: *retetetetetete*. Papi starts looking like a businessman while the clerk starts looking like a bullshitter and before Papi's finger gets to the end of the *retetetetetete* the clerk whistles and a little kid about my age runs out with a cart and starts loading up crates of Country Club raspberry and grape and merengue and orange soda right into the open trunk of Papi's car as Papi caresses my face with his many-ringed hand. Later, the clerk, wearing a grin from ear to ear, will hand me a box with every kind of Country Club yo-yo, and *rututututututu* we take off in Papi's car. I hold on to that box of yo-yos and imagine myself doing tricks with them, making circles in the air and trapping them without getting tangled in the string. Later I imagine myself giving the yo-yos away during recess at my school as the teacher says, Get in line. Everybody wants to be my friend, even Julio César and Raúl wanna be my friends, and they'll teach me all those new swear words in exchange for two, three, or however many yo-yos they want.

four

I fall asleep with my swimsuit on cuz Papi told me he was gonna take me to the beach; I've still got my diving mask on, my swim fins, and water wings on my arms. Papi bought me my swimsuit, which is just a little blue turquoise thong that set Mami's teeth on edge when she saw it. The only thing Papi said was, Didn't they say I was crazy? Well, we'll see what they say now. I put everything on in a rush cuz Papi would be here any minute, at least that's what he said on the phone. I get up super early, before the sun has even come out, and stuff a towel in a bag. When I'm done, I sit down in a mini-rocker custom made just for me that my dad bought for me, of course. I just rock and rock and rock until the phone rings.

It's Papi, who's on his way.

They bring me breakfast on a little tray, bread with cream cheese and milk. But I don't actually swallow anything. I just keep rocking with the tray on my lap. At about ten, they bring me a jar of champola ice cream to refresh me, but I don't actually swallow anything, I just keep rocking with the tray and the jar of champola ice cream. At about noon, they brought some rice with coconut on a plate but I couldn't swallow any of it and I just kept rocking with the little tray, the jar of champola ice cream, and the little plate. I just keep rocking in front of the turned-off TV and I turn the diving mask over so I can look out at the street and see the sun is really intense and the sidewalk looks like it's gonna melt and the trees look like they're gonna melt, and the plate, the jar, and the tray all look like they're gonna melt on me. Mami is taking a nap; I can hear her from here, snoring like the hiss of a snake, but I just keep rocking and rocking until the phone rings.

It's Papi, who's on his way.

When Mami wakes up she brings me a bowl of rice pudding and leaves it at my feet. At five in the afternoon, Mami comes in with a tower of white baby's breath and silver sugar flowers and puts it on my head, and it rocks with my rocking and the bread, the milk, the champola, the rice pudding, the coconut, and me, but I'm not really rocking that much anymore. At seven o'clock Mami opens my mouth with a hydraulic jack and she and a Haitian worker from the construction site across the street whom she's brought over to help her introduce a clear tube which they use to feed me a solution of milk pudding and white pumpkin purée.

All the while, I'm growing really fast and I hear the neighbors say Mami must be spending a fortune on my shoes alone. Since I'm growing so fast, the swimsuit's really tight and makes me turn purple, same with the diving mask, the water wings, and the swim fins. First come the ulcers, then the pustules. The swimsuit disappears amidst my bruises, same with the diving mask, the water wings, and the swim fins. The rice pudding, champola, and everything else begin to rot and fruit flies and ants make castles out of the pumpkins. They bring a priest to reason with me. Certain punishments can be luxurious, the priest says as he sticks his finger in the stinky champola and brings it to his mouth.

I don't rock anymore. The smell of Lycra and blood is marvelous. Sometimes they turn on the TV so I can entertain myself, so I'll forget, but I close my eyes, which are so dry they have to put cotton balls and ice on them.

Don't despair, that's all Mami can say. And I imagine (I'm totally blind now) how my toys are getting old, how ivy and moss are crawling up the walls of my Playmobil fort. But I keep waiting.

And then one day, deep in my ears, I start to hear a little music. At first I thought it was crickets and grasshoppers, the little creatures in my ulcers, or those albino tadpoles, gouramis and tilapias that live in the melted champola, all singing to me, but it was the phone ringing. It's Papi, who's just around the corner.

Then, another day, one of Papi's girlfriends called to say Papi was sick.

And another day, a friend of Papi's called, that Papi had been taken to jail.

And another day, an aunt of Papi's, that Papi had been found dead.

And another day, Papi's sister, that Papi wasn't dead, no way.

And another day it was the operator saying Papi was on the other end and it was a long-distance call.

But I didn't want to, I couldn't, get up. Mami talked to him and told him everything was fine, we were all fine, that I was doing fine in school, that I was exactly like him.

That night a woman came through the window when

we were all sleeping and told me she was very hungry and then, one by one, she ate all the desserts, the sour and bloated milk, the phlegmy rice pudding, the shriveled flan, the rusted sugar flowers, the frosted cotton. She even ate the tadpoles, gouramis, and tilapias, then licked the plates, the glasses, and the bowls until they sparkled even as she took them to the kitchen, where she washed them again and again while singing a little song. I took the feeding tube out myself and got up, limping, until I reached the remote control. It was already dawn, and I hadn't realized so much time had passed that they were talking in English on TV. So now, instead of Our Father, there was instead One two little three little Indians, four little five little six little Indians, seven little eight little nine little Indians, ten little Indian boys and girls. Later, with my head under the pillow, I try to imagine where exactly "just around the corner" Papi might be, and where this corner could be, and what it must take to get around it.

It must require a very big car. Or maybe many cars, one in front of the other.

Then Papi calls and asks, Who do you wanna live with, your dad or your mom? So I say:

car
bicycle
plane
wheel
boat
boot
blue
candy
book
walkie-talkie

run
ball
basketball

Then we started getting cards that said Merry Christmas, Happy Birthday, Happy New Year, Good Luck, Happy Easter, Happy Birthday, It's a Boy!, It's a Girl!, It's a Down Syndrome Martian!, and so on. Cards with clocks, Santa Clauses, elves, hearts, elephants, four-leaf clovers, dinosaurs, trumpets, chimneys, snow, and sometimes little girls, little angels with writing next to them that says, It's You! Cards signed by Papi and one of his girlfriends and one of my new little siblings.

When I don't get cards, I get dolls. Rag dolls, plastic dolls, ceramic dolls. Pierrots, dancers, babies, dolls that drink and shit, dolls that move their teeth, seven black dolls with Afros, blue-eyed dolls that cry when you pull their hair, but also some bald newborns.

And when it's not dolls, it's nannies, young peasants my size with hairy legs, hairy underarms, who go braless and pantyless, who smell like sour oranges and cuaba soap. Mami teaches them how to use a razor and gives them perfume, bras, pantyhose, old lipsticks, and they wear it all on Sundays, when Mami lets them go sit on the garden wall so they can talk to the watchmen and the nannies out in the world. Some of them are nice and tell me stories about drowning women and rolling cabbage heads that aren't really cabbages but human heads. Some let me see the telenovelas and cover my eyes when they kiss on the telenovelas but I see it all anyway cuz they always leave a space between their fingers so I won't miss it. Some show me their tits and, if they're really nice, sometimes even more. Some bathe me with very cold water, saying it's to make me strong. They wait until I have all my Playmobil stuff set up on the floor, ready for battle, the horses and tractors in their places, and then they come with a mop wet with Mistolín to wipe it all away. Almost always, in the end, Mami fires them. Cuz they're thieves, or disgusting, lazy, shameless, meddling, too dark, mixed race, cheap, cuz they say they're from San Cristóbal when they're really from Elías Piña, cuz they stink, have bad breath, fuck watchmen, smoke menthols (whore cigs, not for decent girls), cuz their nipples get erect when people are around, cuz they talk back, use too much bleach, too much oregano, cuz their mother's the biggest of all bitches, cuz they're so damn gutsy, cuz they have such balls, cuz they use razors, perfumes, lipsticks, Mami's new pantyhose.

Where have they gone? Goddammit.

And when it's not the nannies, it's the girlfriends themselves. The sharp little hairs of their recently shaved legs are like cacti on my face. They've made me hide in their pantyhose. So Mami won't see me, so Papi's other girlfriends won't see me. They disguise themselves as female cops, as Mami's college classmates, as waitstaff, as young girls on their way to the store wearing shorts and strapless blouses; one even dressed up as a kindergarten teacher and hurried off with me and my lunch box and my little backpack screaming, MA ME MI MO MU, PA PE PI PO PU, SA SE SI SO SU! until another one—this one disguised as Mami—cut her off screaming, TA TE TI TO TU, RA RE RI RO RU! and snatched me from her arms in one fell swoop (my lunch box opens in midair and everything pours out of it: the milk from the thermos, the cheese sticks, the hard-boiled egg). The teachers, the teachers' friends, and the parents who come to pick up their children are left SPEECHLESS.

Now they kidnap me from my own home, right in front of Mami, but she doesn't see a thing. They come at me on the TV, they talk to me on the radio with their pantyhose voices, with their pantyhose mouths, with their suits made of pantyhose, and they just pantyhose right in my face. They take me to their apartments, to their apartment hotels (which Papi pays for in advance), and they bathe me in their tubs filled with berry-scented bubbles. They make one of the servants, just one of them (who Papi pays for in advance), bring fried yucca with ketchup and a vanilla malt on a tray for me right to the tub. They let me paint my nails, they let me jump on the bed, they let me break the bed, they buy me a new bed every day just so I can break it (later they tell Papi he's the one breaking them so he'll continue to pay for them in advance). When I'm constipated, they smear me with Vaseline and pluck out the turds with the long red nails all my dad's girlfriends have.

When it's not the girlfriends, then it's her Papi sends, the Cuban, with a document that says she's the one, that Mami should pack my bag and hand me over, that I'm finally gonna be reunited with my father but Mami doesn't trust it (given all those costume changes) and has Dr. Lerux (Dr. Lerux is very old) take a look at the document, but she still doesn't trust it (given all that kidnapping) and she has Dr. Bisonó look over Dr. Lerux before he looks at the document, but Mami still doesn't trust it (given how the world is) and has Dr. Jiminían look over Dr. Bisonó and his entire genealogical tree before he looks over Dr. Lerux and so forth to infinity. Before I can take a plane to see Papi, a mob of doctors stick speculums into each other in our living room and the Cuban and I discuss whether or not I should take my little stuffed bee named Maya.

We finally leave. I'm very happy and Mami dries a tear as we go out on the tarmac. I'm wearing a yellow linen dress and the sun is splendid. Little Playmobil cars carry our bags, zigging left and zagging right, and when I get to the first step of the airstairs, I turn around and say good-bye, even though there's no one and nothing on the tarmac, just yellow and white stripes, but I know Mami is waving her hand to say good-bye somewhere out there, surrounded by a coterie of doctors (all of them very old and really into examining each other) who pat her shoulder and tell her this is gonna be very good for both of us.

Now that I'm calmer and the plane has taken off and the Cuban has explained why I had to buckle my seat belt, I realize she's the most beautiful woman I've ever seen in my life. I hear a voice that says, The most beautiful woman I've ever seen in my life. Later she tells me I'm very pretty and I vomit all over her. A flight attendant came right away to clean up the mess. Just before leaving with the dirty rags she gave me a little bag in case the Cuban told me I was pretty again. Then the flight attendant winked at me, which is what Papi's girlfriends do when they're in disguise and they want me to know it's them.

The Cuban, who has very soft hands with short nails painted the same light polish as Papi, puts her arm around me and now the silk of her blouse is the most delicious fabric that has ever touched me in my life. I lean my head on her chest and she caresses my hair and it's then I feel we're flying and I understand we are thousands upon thousands of feet from my rocker, my games, between my mom and me, and as I close my eyes somebody paints a smile on my face.

I'm shoved around and around and it's the Cuban who's shoving me. When I wake up, she's dressed in camouflage, a green beret on her head. She has a cigar in her mouth and wears a fake beard and I wonder what she's supposed to be disguised as now. The Cuban is threatening the flight attendant against the bathroom door, giving her little cuts with a sky-blue plastic knife. Later she makes her way through the cabin using a nail cutter. The passengers cooperate cuz they've all read in travel magazines how Cuban terrorists force planes to land in Cuba with the intention of picking up dissidents. So we cooperate, all very quietly. When the plane lands in Havana, I go up to the window and see how the Cuban, fixing her loose beard, helps some schoolgirls in Pioneer uniforms get down from a truck and go into the cargo hold, all of them very beautiful, all of them for Papi, which is really (never better expressed) something else.

When I wake up again, I'm in a room I don't recognize. I get up and my feet are surprised by the carpeting. I go out to the hallway and the air smells of newness, of how things smell when they first come out of the box, like Barbies. I liven up and rub my eyes with my knuckles, then look for another door to open.

Maybe this is New York or Miami.

Maybe this is Papi's house.

I opened a door and the only thing I could see on the bed with black sheets was a shoulder covered by strands of brown hair. I wanted to touch that shoulder and for the person to whom that shoulder belonged, who was naked and sleeping facedown next to my father, to turn around, without waking up too much, and kiss my mouth. I've never wanted anything so much in my life.

That shoulder covered by strawberry-scented hair was calling to me. I kept gazing at it from the door and then from the edge of my dad's bed, and then I got so close I could almost touch the strands and the shoulder with my nose. But I could feel vomit pushing at my throat, which is why I left the room, and then my nausea immediately went away. In the living room I turned on the TV Papi had bought the day before, which was enormous. I stood next to the thing, pressing the channel button with my finger (my nail was dirty) but I wasn't looking at the screen. When I finally focused, it was Jimmy Swaggart's show, the same one I used to watch with my mom in the DR, in which people ditch their crutches and shout, Hallelujah! I like how people say hallelujah and now that there was no translation and Jimmy spoke only in English, the only thing I understood were the hallelujahs. I thought if I understood the hallelujahs it was cuz I understood English. So I thought: Hallelujah. And I said: Hallelujah. That's when I felt María Cristina (my dad's Cuban girlfriend), her arms surrounding me. She put her lips very close to my ear and asked, What are you doing, crazy girl?

Back then, I was really little, and I got even smaller so María Cristina could pick me up off the floor and kiss my neck, my cheek, my eyes, my belly, lifting up my Spider-man PJs.

I let it happen. I just let it happen.

Later, María Cristina and I turn on MTV and, since she knows more English than me, she teaches me the lyrics to the songs I like. There's one I like a lot that goes like this, Let's hear it for the boy, ah, let's give the boy a hand, eh yeah, ehhh, yeah. It's American music. American music. María Cristina and I dance and dance and dance, and now no one can take our MTV away from us, no one can take our MTV. Before we go out, María Cristina and I shower together and comb our hair together and she teaches me how to match my clothes, especially given all the clothes

Papi bought us. She says I have to learn all this so no one will call me a hick like they did to her when she first got here. She arrived in a boat crammed with people. I imagine her about my size, wearing a white cheesecloth dress and staring at the sea. María Cristina. She tells me this story every night at bedtime. She comes in the room she and Papi have prepped for me, with two beds in case one of my friends stays the night, a yellow table between the two little beds and a light that shines orange on the pillows and sheets. She covers me with the blanket and lays down on her side next to me, a leg over me. I feel the weight of her leg and smell the strawberries in her hair and, in the dark, I use a finger to feel the thickness of one of her eyebrows.

María Cristina lets me crack eggs for a cake, but I don't do it right, so she lets me try again. Three times. María Cristina lets me wear her sunglasses and chew ten pieces of gum at the same time. When we go to the supermarket, I get in the front part of the cart cuz I'm too big for the little rack. María Cristina pushes hard and jumps on the cart so the two of us roll down the aisle and stick our tongues out at the old woman in shorts with a walker who's standing in front of the Quaker oatmeal section. We also stick our tongues out at the squatting Puerto Rican who puts price stickers on the sardines. Then we stared at another old woman talking to the ninety-nine-cent cans of powdered milk, for Christ's sake. María Cristina takes my hand to cross the street and I don't let go. In my mind, I don't let go of the new words she's taught me either.

And now to count to twenty.

All this happens on Saturdays and Sundays cuz the rest of the week there's a babysitter who comes to pick lice off me. She's not Cuban but Venezuelan, but she's also Papi's girlfriend. Papi told her I had a lot of lice, that I was covered, and that they had to go. The lice came home on my head. I got them at school, and even after they'd all died on every other kid's head, they were still having a party on mine. The teachers had a blast killing them. It got me out of all kinds of homework: subtraction, addition, writing "my mom loves me" one hundred times. Thanks to those blessed lice, the teachers were quite entertained. One day, one teacher even brought a book in which she compared my lice (fat like little beans) with the ones in the book. Mine sprouted on my hair and skated on the curls. Then Mami said it might have been better if I'd had bad hair. She prayed my hair would turn bad, like on black people, so the lice would get tangled in an Afro and choke. I could hear them singing and dancing at all hours, drunk on my sweet blood, and I'd scratch myself with both hands. Sometimes I'd even ask my friends to please help me scratch.

That's why they buzzed my hair off, like a boy's.

And that's why when we play that we're mom and dad, my friends want me to play dad.

And that's why I climbed on top of Natasha under her bed.

(Same with Mónica and Sunyi and Renata and Jessy and Franchy and Zunilda and Ivecita.)

And that's why Doña Victoria, Natasha's grandmother, whipped her with a belt.

(And Paola and Lily and Sandrita and Gabi and Julia and Karina.)

That's why Mami started dressing me only in dresses.

(And Verónica and Claudia and Laurita.)

And that's why when I ran and fell, I scraped my legs and knees.

(And Katy and Daniela and Ana María.)

And that's why I got two scabs on my knees.

(And Nicole and Charo and Carla Patricia.)

And that's why Mami started dressing me only in pants.

(And Larissa and Fénix and Lisa and Consuelo and Aimée and Melissa.)

But the lice kept sucking my blood.

The babysitter is totally clear about this. She washes my hair with something Papi bought that itches more than the lice, and later she dries my hair with the blower on high so as to fry the lice. When she's finished, she heats up a can of Chef Boyardee and my charred ears fall into my plate of spaghetti and meatballs.

In the afternoon, we go to the condo pool, which is full of kids of all sizes and colors who chase and push each other and climb on each other's shoulders, all the while holding Luke Skywalker and Darth Vader action figures in their hands. I love to sit on the edge of the pool before going in and watching as folks who arrive dive in headfirst or roll up their bodies into cannonballs and splash water everywhere. Some dare to use the diving board, performing mortal leaps and then belly flop or fall on their backs. When they climb up the ladder from the water, they itch so much they twist their bodies like lizards. I scream at them: SÓBATE QUE NO HAY BENGUÉ. And somebody else falls on his face and I scream: SÓBATE QUE NO HAY BENGUÉ. They scream things back at me I don't understand cuz, though some of them are younger than me, they already know more English than the devil.

All of a sudden a blond kid who's been jumping off the diving board a while gets sick of hearing me scream SÓBATE QUE NO HAY BENGUÉ and gives me the finger. Back in my country, back in my school, I had already found out what that means. Raúl and Julio César told me that if I showed them my panties, they'd explain it. We went behind a bus to make the deal but I can barely form the gesture with my own hand and sometimes I leave too many fingers out, so what I can't say with my fingers I say with my mouth: YO MOTHAFUCKA SONOFABITCH GO FUCK YO OWN SELF. The blond kid motions to another kid, this one in a green bathing suit, who tells him: She says you're an SOB. The blond kid, who's sitting on the diving board dangling his legs, starts to get red in the face and the drops of pool water on his body evaporate and his freckles get real daaaaaaark and his veins (there are veins) engorge just like this one friend of Manuel Moretta's.

The blond kid is throwing paralyzing daggers at me. He's gonna jump from the diving board onto my neck and drown me. Next to the fence, my babysitter is fixing her G-string while she talks to the lifeguard. They don't know they're gonna kill me, that I'm gonna wind up choking on water and chemicals (they taste so bad). But a muscular arm pops up out of the pool (under the diving board, under the blond kid), an arm with a hard bicep (which we could see from afar) comes out of the water like the dead in that Michael Jackson video where they stick their arms out of their graves. The arm grabs one of the blond kid's legs and pulls and pulls and pulls and drags him to the deep blue where there's a little sign that says 18 Feet.

From up here we see a writhing black mass as the grisly sun lights the surface of the water. The rest of the kids run home but a few stay quiet like me, just looking down. Still next to the fence, the lifeguard fixes the G-string on my babysitter.

The blond kid comes up, pops his head out of the water, and we can see his tears, his boogers disappearing into the pool water. He wails loudly and gets out of the pool and hugs his belly all the way home. I feel a bit sorry for him. The owner of the arm remains below, like a brown stain, like a toad. The babysitter comes up carrying a towel and makes me start walking away. Turning toward the pool the whole time, I ask her if she noticed what was going on and she says, Yeah, kiddo, that lifeguard was drooling all over me.

That night the Cubans come to play Monopoly with Papi. The Cubans play with real money. There are three of them, a young man and two old guys who smoke cigars and spit on Papi's rug. They wear bracelets and gold chains that are thicker than Papi's. When I go give them some snacks María Cristina has prepared for them, the oldest guy tells me I have a star. I look for it on my clothes as if it was a stain, and he laughs. *Ha ha ha.* He twists the thickest ring on his finger. Papi laughs and tells a lot of jokes as he plays and the Cubans practically pee in their pants from laughing so hard. Later, I sit on Papi's lap when he throws the dice and they fall on Paseo Tablado, so he very quickly buys a chain of condos and hotels. Each building Papi puts up is named after someone in his family—Leysi I, Leysi II, and Leysi III, after his younger sister, Apartment Hotel Cilí, after his mother, and in one of China's hotels, a restaurant called Cristi's, after his other sister. There's a street named after me and an avenue and an airport named after Papi.

I feel optimistic, Papi tells the eldest Cuban as he shoves a snack in his mouth. I ask Papi what optimistic means, and as he licks the sweet-and-sour sauce from his finger, he tells me it means being an SOB.

One afternoon, María Cristina asks me to go with her to the supermarket, and as I run after her I pass the pool and see the dark toad down in the deep end. When we come back with the grocery bags (I help with the one that has the bananas), the stain is still down there. That night, Papi throws a barbecue at the pool and as we're preparing everything (I help with the tablecloth), the pool lights come on and the stain slowly rises, like a siren. The stain nears the pool ladder, the arm emerges and holds on; it's the muscular arm of a boy with very strong arms. He's very wet and has black hair that's a little too long. María Cristina greets him, Hi, Kiki. Kiki holds himself up with both hands on the ladder and then jumps and jumps and jumps with his single leg until he reaches María Cristina, who smiles and hands him a can of Coke. I was born this way, Kiki tells me as Papi's friends start arriving at the pool accompanied by women in bikinis. They're young and old and hold their beer cans with their little fingers up in the air like an antenna, and they dance merengue without letting go of those cans. Even I dance. Kiki dances with his crutches. The music is very loud and everyone is very happy, drinking and eating bits of meat from Papi's barbecue. He is wearing a green apron with yellow letters that say #1 Master as he stokes the fire. A few of Papi's friends are playing a game in which they throw their Bulova watches into the deepest part of the pool to see who gets to them first.

When all my lice have died off, they're gonna take me to Disney World, I tell Kiki. I'm gonna meet Mickey and Goofy. Are there people inside those Mickey Mouses and Donald Ducks? I don't know, I don't think so, says Kiki. Later he recommends that when all my lice are dead I should go to Epcot Center, the center of the universe. Then Papi hurries us back in the house cuz, as he tells us with his mouth on his beer as if he were kissing it, this is no longer kid-friendly. On the TV, Charlie Brown is in a spelling bee, and whenever someone misspells a word their heads explode like balloons and go *pop*, tauromachy, *pop*, *pop*, lugubriously, *pop*, outlandish.

Pop.

Papi wakes me up by jerking the sheet off in a single move, like those people that remove tablecloths without touching the dishes. He drags me over to the pool where the party is still going on. I don't understand anything. A black woman in a bikini clings to Papi's hip and sucks on his chest hair. María Cristina makes a face and Papi pulls her back and sticks her on his free hip. María Cristina makes another face and Papi whispers in her ear: We're gonna have fun, mamita, and then he arranges the G-string on the black woman.

Later, as he squeezes the two of them by the waist, Papi raises his voice and declares: Now my daughter will sing something for us that she's prepared.

You all are the audience and so I take my time. You guys are the audience and when I make like I'm gonna open my mouth, you freeze like a bunch of rocks, just waiting for time to pass, but I'm the time that's gonna go right by you, like a song, like a miracle of light that's gonna turn this time back, to before, to a time that can be counted again in seconds and minutes and breaks along with the applause, like a river of gravel and marbles, like a million maracas made from all those watches.

You guys are like that, a little dumb, a bit sardonic, cynical, paunchy, with puffy cheeks, critical, fanatical, cruel, capable of a love that forgives everything and makes everything greater. With such bad taste, and without it, with so many gold chains and girlfriends that you can't even see them anymore—you, his girlfriends, and his attire are all the same thing, a dark sea before me. I'm the only one illuminated, the only one receiving this white light from the round point at the back of the space, which signals to me and follows me on the stage. Sometimes a light winks from the black sea like a phosphorescent fish. Sometimes it's one, two, three lights at the same time.

I still haven't left my dressing room. I'm still lit by the little bulbs on the frame of the mirror where I've put photos of my Papi, me and my Papi when he was still alive and would carry me like a little purse, with my legs around his waist and my arms crossed on his shoulder. Behind us in one of the photos the dolphins at the Miami Seaquarium jump in the air for a can of salmon. I kiss the photo and cross myself. I pull closer the ice bucket that's cooling a bottle of champagne I wanna suck on, and get up. I'm surrounded by black silk blouses, seventeen of them, and black gabardine slacks which a black woman with an iron has creased so sharply that they could cut through metal like a Japanese knife.

I go to touch the crease with my finger but pull back immediately as if I'd just been burned and then say, with a voice that isn't mine, Impressive.

I pull the hangers and proceed. First the pants and then the blouse. When I'm all buttoned up someone comes to dust me off and pulls a hair off with pincers.

I zip up my pants, the zipper stuttering along. Outside, an impatient murmur has degenerated into a million feet hitting the floor and hands clapping on the beat. They want my head. They have one, two fingers, in their mouths to whistle and spray spit and make noise. I imagine faces and hands marking this or that whistle and in the midst of all that gluttonous screaming I see the jowls, hands, rings, fake fingernails, the teeth in the exaggerated smiles of those outside who are screaming, almost as if they'd rehearsed it: IF YOU DON'T COME OUT NOW, THIS PLACE IS GONNA GO UP IN FLAMES, IF YOU DON'T COME OUT NOW, THIS PLACE IS GONNA GO UP IN FLAMES!

I stick a piece of ice in my mouth and chew. When my teeth finish crunching, an invisible orchestra starts playing string and wind instruments and when the people hear the first note, they begin to bleed from their noses. They shake each other by the shoulders, their eyes blank, they vomit on each other, throw their crutches in the air, get sick, shit, kick, elbow, and then they all stand up at the same time to receive me.

HERE I COME. HERE I COME. HERE I AM dragging Papi's pants (which they hemmed with staples but that still cover my rubber sandals), Papi's silk shirt (which doesn't do much to keep this wind from going right through me), and blue Magic Marker sideburns and mustache. I keep quiet as the music continues, so you guys shut up as if for all eternity, as if you'd died, and listen to what I have to say.

I'm the one who follows you each night, who has no life other than pursuing you . . .

The pool reflects an interstellar light as I lip-synch Raphael's hit song and hold a hairbrush like a mic. I can make out Papi's girlfriends' bodies, which struggle to keep the floats and the inflatable toys all in one corner of the pool to make room so they can improvise a synchronized dance number. No one moves out of the water. Papi's sitting in a chaise lounge with María Cristina on his lap. Her eyes look at me with a sparkle, those eyes that sparkle like they always do, like fireworks.

The one who waits for you, who dreams of you, who prays every night for your love . . .

I make the same moves I've made one hundred times in front of the mirror: I close a fist, extend an arm as if carrying a tray, lift my chin, close my eyes, nod with my jaw. I imagine Papi and Mami have died so my eyes will moisten as if I'm about to cry (I always get this right). People just drool, though their faces show panic. And as soon as Spain's Raphael sings "Yo soy aquel" through me again, I start to come down from the stage, which is actually a Plexiglas patio table with the umbrella removed.

At first, I come down very slowly so I won't fall, but I never stop making my gestures, I never stop lip-synching, and it isn't until I get to the floor that I look at her.

She returns my gaze. And I look at her some more. In my mind, Papi and Mami's coffins descend simultaneously and I keep two whole tears right on the edge of my eyelids. I continue staring at María Cristina as I come closer, slowly, and as I get so I could almost touch her nose with mine . . .

And I'm here, here, to love you.

And I'm here, here, to adore you,

And I'm here, here, to ask you for . . .

Then I grab her hand and put my arm around her waist and with the other I hold on to the ladder that Kiki has dropped down from the silent ship drifting in the air over my show and which we've stolen from one of the guests. Kiki maneuvers to get some height and María Cristina and I quickly lift off the ground, away from Papi, while we kiss with our eyes closed. I'm so strong that my eight-year-old arm holds us both while, below, all of Papi's girlfriends' legs hover over the luminous water to complete their dance and Raphael's voice finishes without my lip-synching: *Loooooooove, looooooove, looooooove.*

five

This is the only thing that can be heard: Papi and his business associates, divvying everything up, thousand-peso bills, winning lottery tickets, watches, chains, plastic bags filled with gold jewelry, Porsche-brand corkscrews, thousands of millions of five-peso bills, one for you, one for me. The loose change gets thrown to the trees.

Papi's friends all have little bellies and mustaches and gold watches just like Papi's. They talk to you as if they're using walkie-talkies, even when you're right next to them. Papi and the guys hug each other a lot and slap each other's backs with open hands, especially when they've sold a car or two to your damn mother and they split the bills on Papi's desk, one for you, one for me. Almost all of Papi's friends are older than him, except Puchy, but Puchy isn't really Papi's friend. Even though Papi gave him a gold watch as a present, Puchy is more like his assistant.

It wasn't that long ago that Puchy was taking my clothes and borrowing my bike, but now he wears suits like Papi, and shoes and chains like Papi, and Papi even lends him cars. Before Puchy had his license, he and I would crawl into a couple of cars parked at Papi's dealership, Puchy in a black Porsche and me in a brown Jaguar, and we'd pretend we were racing side by side, screeching through our teeth to make like brakes, our fists closed tight on the steering wheels, our arms straight like sticks, our backs pushing the seat back as if we were going really fast, so much faster than anyone else.

But now Puchy races for real and when Papi tells him to take me for a drive, Puchy leans on the accelerator and the car takes off like it's gonna fly. Puchy has cassettes scattered all over Papi's car. He puts one in, poking a finger in my chest as he sings, Do you come from the land down under? I get excited and laugh, although inside I'm really annoyed cuz there's still some time to go before I can drive for real and put in my own cassettes and sing, I'm a backdoor man. I pass Puchy and lower my window to say, *Ciiiiiiiiiao*, love, and let the last phrase of the song I'm singing fill his car.

Puchy is gonna be a partner very soon. To be Papi's partner, all he needs is a girlfriend, and one day he'll have her and no one will be able to stop him, with his blond girlfriend, his Mercedes, and his ring as fat as a Hershey's Kiss.

Milly got a store. Papi got it for her. He sent Milly with one thousand dollars to Miami to get the merchandise to sell in the store, but she spent half in one week with her friends on three-hundred-dollar rehydrating creams and five-hundred-dollar massages. She spent the other half on perfumes. Papi had to send one of his associates to go get her and he told Papi that Milly was camping it up, getting into some real mariconería. I get confused about certain words. I mean, I don't understand them very well. First of all, *associate*. I think it's like saying "pal," that is, like when Papi baptizes his associates' babies and then his associates' kids come and stick their hands in his pocket and pull out two or three bills as a way of greeting him. Papi's business associates have their own pockets but I never go pull anything out of them cuz I know if it even occurred to me, Papi would smack me something fierce. The other word is *mariconería*.

When Milly came back from her trip, Papi shut himself in his office with her and they didn't let me come in. When Milly emerged, she was wearing a suit just like Papi's and a ring and spinning a BMW keychain on one finger. The only thing she needed to be one of Papi's business associates was a girlfriend. Then there'll be no stopping her.

Now Puchy and Milly look exactly alike, with their suits, their rings, their chains, their cassettes scattered all over the floor of the car. Music blasting. And cologne so intense that people faint (*plop*) as if they'd just seen a ghost when they pass by. They have boots, tennis racquets, golf clubs, basketballs, surfboards, skateboards—each one has his and her own rugs and leopard-skin furniture cuz Papi bought both of them their own apartment. The twins flank Papi when he goes out now, and both wear their hair cut this way: bangs and a long, thin braid that drops down from the back of their neck, and a sweep of hair, a little wavy, which covers one eye. Sometimes they add a blond streak. They wear white double-breasted suits with white upholstered buttons. Papi, in the middle, always wears gray, a pearl-gray down to his shoes.

Papi attracts cars, famous people, people who wanna invest in our country. So people bring him gifts, ask him for advice, buy him cars, give him the keys to one. As soon as Papi came back, people were over to visit, stinky poor people Papi introduced to me as he hugged them:

This guy taught me how to drive, this guy how to dance. Papi takes them to his office and hears out these stinky people and their majestic plans that entail Papi lending them money so they can buy a minivan and turn it into a taxi and make enough money in a month to buy another minivan and then another the next month (these stinky people then pull out a napkin on which they've scrawled their calculations for gas and fares) so that in a year these stinky people will have a public transportation network and pay Papi back double what he lends them. Papi listens while staring at his impeccable cuticles, and later, a secretary brings them coffee and they give the stinky guy a cap with Papi's logo on it and they drop the subject of the loan (Papi pats the guy's back as he sends him off with twenty pesos).

The day Papi came back the stinky people had already formed a line in the parking lot of my abuela Cilí's building. Papi dressed like a purse snatcher so he could get through the crowd without being recognized, but they were already building cardboard houses in the parking lot and cutting down jabilla trees for kindling to cook rice with herring. The next morning, Papi went out on the balcony in his underwear and told them to go home, that everybody was gonna get what they deserved and not to despair.

The first thing Papi did when he got home was open his suitcases. The twins and I were waiting, sitting very calmly like good boys and girls. China, Leysi, and Cilí all hug Papi, kissing him on the mouth every time he pulls out another gift. Cilí whispers to Papi: Don't forget about yours. So Papi tears a sheet from a yellow pad, licks the tip of a pencil and starts making a list, one hundred for that one, and two hundred for that other one, one hundred for that other one. Cilí looks over his shoulder to make sure everybody's name is on the list. Money, freezers, cars, even houses for old time's sake.

Papi's making his list but it's never ending. He shows it to China or Leysi and they say, Remember Don Chichí and Sergeant Alegría, or, Aren't you gonna add the late Evarista's orphans to that list? Papi keeps making the list. One hundred dollars for you, one hundred for you, one hundred for you, and one hundred for you. He writes all the names and asks that we each make him a list of the people we think should be included. And then everybody on that list will be asked for their own list. Papi doesn't wanna forget anybody.

I'm gonna go to a hotel, Papi tells Cilí. Papi needs more room to receive all these people. I'm gonna buy a house, Papi tells Cilí. So Papi buys a house and an apartment and a vacant lot where he parks all the cars he brought back to sell. By the next day they're already airing a commercial and that day Papi's on TV shaking hands with another satisfied customer and their grip is so tight it looks like their hands might break. Papi already has a secretary, two secretaries who answer the phone and arrange lists in alphabetical order or by importance or they don't arrange squat and go out with Puchy to buy cashew sweets they eat in the car, high heels off as they wiggle their toes in front of the AC vent.

Now, for greater efficiency, they've installed an answering machine in which Papi's voice says he's not there, to leave a message after the beep. The first thing Papi does when he gets to his office at about eleven is take two Rapidita hangover-helper pills with a glass of milk and punch the button to hear the long list of messages in which the stinky people, his business associates, his kin, his intimates, the media, his clients, and his girlfriends get shriller and shriller. Papi sits down at his desk, takes the remote, and turns the TV to any old channel. Later, with both elbows on the desk, he puts an index finger to each temple and twirls them around. The twins fly about behind his chair like angels over a Christmas manger.

When Papi moves his fingers like that, he's actually making money. It doesn't work for me. I put my fingers on my temples and nothing happens. But it does for Papi. It's really something to see: how when Papi puts his fingers on his temples somebody comes in right away and they meet, and then, when Papi and I are alone again, he says, I'm turning you into a millionaire. Then we go out to eat with one of Papi's girlfriends at some fine restaurant and I order pizza and he asks me why he should bother to bring me to such a place if I'm gonna order pizza. The girlfriend, who's a total brownnoser, takes my side and the two of us hit the table with our forks and knives and yell, *Pizza! Pizza! Pizza!*

The pizza arrives and we start eating it, first burning our tongues on the cheese, then leaving the crust on the plate cuz neither Papi nor I eat it and his girlfriend is such an asskisser that she doesn't either. During dessert, Papi grabs his girlfriend's finger and shows me her ring, which boasts a diamond the size of a wad of gum. We're getting married, the girlfriend announces, next Saturday.

Papi puts his fingers on his temples (the people in the restaurant think it's cuz he has a headache) and begins generating money and houses and decorators dragging fabric samples, paint samples, tile samples. Papi's girlfriend tells the black guys to bring this, take that. If you break something, you'll pay for it, she tells them, and then she closes her fist and the wad-of-gum-sized diamond shoots out a deafening ray that checks the chosen color or fabric or tile at a distance, striking the painters, construction workers, and decorators if she doesn't aim right. Papi's fingers on his temples produce suits and dresses, pedicures and manicures for all the guests, and the costs of six buses with waitstaff to transfer the guests to the farm that Papi, with his fingers on his skull right this minute, is generating to take the architect who designed the house by the river, and the wood and cement and the farmworkers (each with a family). We are still at the fine restaurant when Papi (his fingers now making such tight circles that it looks like he's boring holes into his red temples) conjures the last three horses of the twenty-five he's gonna keep on the farm.

The wedding day arrives and Papi and his girlfriend get married. But before they can sign and the bride's makeup can run cuz of her tears, the photographer takes pictures of the couple at the pool, coming down the stairs, petting a horse, holding a glass of champagne, with the groom's family, with the bride's family, with both families surrounding the seven-layer cake, with the couple's mothers, one of the bride with the twins, of the groom's daughter, of the seven-layer cake. Later, they make wallet-sized copies of the best photo for everyone. Papi's bride writes an affectionate message on the back. I put a number on it and arrange it with the other photos of Papi's other weddings, held together like baseball cards with a green rubber band.

Every Friday, the school bus drops me off at Papi's dealership cuz Mami doesn't have a car. Mami can't even drive and she sends me to school on the bus. The bus driver's name is Siboney and he's a thick-lipped black man with teeth as stubby as fingers. Four-Eyes! he says to me every time I get on the bus and every time he sees me in the rearview mirror. Juan José is in the second seat and he calls me an overgrown mosquito. Three seats back, there's Damián, who says I'm a mini-witch and later (when we're closer) they call me Skinny-Whinny, Failure to Thrive, Heron, Biafran Baby, Spaghetti Noodle, María Palito, Old Bat, Giraffe, Palo e Lu, Electric Post, Lucy Leap and Throw, Water Hose, Brittle, Baller. Let me check, says Papi's secretary when I step into the AC and she lets Papi know I'm here, and I hear Papi's voice saying how many times does he have to tell her that she doesn't have to announce me.

Sometimes Papi is at a business dinner and when I get there the secretary orders me a pizza. I sit in Papi's office and run through all the cable channels. At about six, Papi calls and tells the secretary to put me in a taxi to my mom's house cuz the meeting is going long.

Sometimes Papi takes me with him to his business dinners, which are at restaurants where his business associates order lobster and tear them apart without the aid of pliers. They laugh harder than everybody else in the restaurant and spit pieces of shellfish at my glasses. They guffaw and hit the table with their fists and loosen the belts on their pants when they're through eating. When a young girl who doesn't wear a bra yet walks by, they say, Oh what little nips, and Papi says, The Niña, Pinta, and Santa María, so they'll remember I'm present, so they'll remember I also have nips. That's when they cough into their napkins and change the subject and then they talk about their pals' wives, about their pals' wives' daughters, and how much those daughters look like them, and that's about when a spit-covered chickpea lands on my glasses.

They're looking at the dessert menu while I stare at the

girl with the nips, who's about my age and stares back at me from her table. Her mom and dad are arguing, threatening each other with spoons. I get up and go to the bathroom and she follows me. Once there, I tell her that when I was really little, I got a growth on my nipple about the size of a pigeon pea and they cut it off using local anesthesia. I remember how the little growth fell on the stainless steel that made me so cold. Later, I kept losing layers, cuz the doctor had wrapped half of my chest with gauze and Band-Aids and bandages, and the bandages kept falling as if they were leaves from a tree.

When Papi's girlfriends find out about my surgical procedure and my convalescence, they order pizzas for me and send photos of their Winnie-the-Pooh rings, which are, hey, diamonds. They send me gifts, invite me to the movies. Mami throws the gifts away without even opening them. The kids from the neighborhood wait around for Mami to throw them out so they can pick them up, but then their moms throw them out cuz the kids aren't supposed to play in the trash. In the end, the neighborhood kids agree to gather the gifts and bury them rather than take them home, marking the place with a cross. The dirt in the little park on the corner is so loose from the digging that just about anything would sprout: corn, beans, potatoes, cassava, yams so big and hard they've twisted and broken the rusty playground swings. Papi's girlfriends are worthless. They call me, and they write me letters. Mami burns them; Mami pulls her hair out and tells Papi, You'd better figure out what you're gonna to do. When Papi leaves them, or when they say he's dumped them (some don't even know him), they call me in tears and tell me they spent the wee hours having an abortion to get rid of one of Papi's babies so that I'll give them

Papi's private personal phone number, which Papi has told me not to give to anyone. But I give it to them and Papi changes numbers and doesn't give me the new one cuz I sided with his girlfriends.

On Fridays Siboney's bus drops me off at Papi's dealership. Siboney calls after me: In the shade, Four-Eyes, in the shade. But on the sidewalk on Avenida Abraham Lincoln there's not even a little smudge of shade (go ahead and try cuz you're not gonna find it). Damián, Juan José, and all the other shorties, balls of fat, balls of boogers, balls of bait, shitty asses, panty chewers, cocksuckers, suck-what-you-finds, stick their heads out the bus windows like turtles so they can see the BMWs and the Ferraris Papi has in the parking lot. Today is his birthday but Papi doesn't like to celebrate birthdays (who wants to celebrate the birth of a poor boy on a dirt floor, says Papi). Mami has bought a gift for me to give to Papi, a pair of Hawaiian shorts for the beach, since Papi goes to the beach so much. I already know Papi's gonna ask me if I picked them out and if I say it was Mami he's gonna say, Man, they're so ugly. So I feel a certain joy as the gift box gets bashed around in my backpack all day long.

As soon as I arrive, Papi's secretary tells me he's not there and hasn't left instructions about ordering me a pizza. In the meantime, the secretary pulls a Tupperware out of a drawer and divvies up some chicken locrio into two plates, one for me and one for her. When we're finished eating she lets me in to Papi's office, which is jammed with gifts: floral arrangements, a cake shaped like a machine gun, freezers, jewels. I sit among the gifts and the congratulatory notes, all that expensive chocolate just for me. I turn on the TV and raise my feet to the desk as I lift the top off the first box of bonbons. When the secretary tells me via intercom that someone's sent a "special" present for Papi, I tell her to send it in and then a bosomy bikini-clad clown comes through Papi's office door. She climbs on the desk in her heels and gets on all fours to sing "Happy Birthday" to me while rubbing her tits on the remote control in my hand. I'm so scared the bonbons melt in my mouth.

When the clown leaves, I tell the secretary, I'm not in for anyone, and I stay by myself in the office for a long time. I turn off the TV and go over the place without getting up from the chair, which has wheels. I use my feet to push off, like with oars. I pause in front of the mural behind the desk, a palm-filled landscape with buildings and lights and Mercedes-Benz logos and what looks like a river of tomato sauce coming out of one of the windows of the Mercedes. To the left of the mural, there's a door that leads to a black-tiled bathroom. I slither in without getting out of the chair. The bathroom is my favorite part of Papi's office, with its black tub and faucets shaped like dragons. I get up from the chair and turn on the faucet to waste some soap, as Cilí would say, pushing the button so the green liquid falls in my hands like a monster's mucous. Next to the sink there's a smaller door that leads to the sauna, where a few weeks ago I covered the walls with Vicksvaporoo cuz Papi asked me to. I went in with a jar of Vicks and smeared the cedar walls with gobs of the mentholated goo. Papi later told me that when he was little they used to rub it on his chest every night so he'd breathe better.

Although the office, the bathroom, and the sauna are very insulated, you can still hear the noise from the avenue and the impertinent speakers on the cars filing past the dealership to see the silver Porsches, the red Ferraris, and the little black Audis Papi has parked outside. I can hear the motors of each car driving by and the owners of those cars mentally turning on the ignition of Papi's cars. Tomorrow they'll go and hock everything so they can buy a car from Papi and then they'll blast off at a million miles an hour down Avenida Lincoln to the Malecón, to the reefs, to the bottom of the sea, where the sharks will bust their teeth on so much metal.

According to his business associates, Papi has a bear's hug when it comes to buying and a tiger's caress for selling. Papi's getting ahead, and his associates with him, so far ahead so fast that you can hardly see him anymore. Hardly anybody sees him anymore. He always keeps the fastest car for himself, and there's a curtain of smoke wherever he goes, turning him into smoke. A cloud of smoke. Next to the bench in the sauna there's another smaller door, but it's not visible at first sight. You have to stick your fingers in a cleft in the wood to realize there's a secret entrance, which I discovered thanks to the Vicksvaporoo. I open it and hear everybody launching their sports cars off the Malecón. You have to get on your knees here. I go inside this little room, in which Papi and me and one other person might fit in a fetal position. At the very bottom there's the smallest of all doors, and it has a combination lock.

six

Papi and I are going to hell in a handbag. We're on the highway! Papi corrects me: The highway! We're listening to music, reciting the numbers and letters of the license plates on the cars we pass as if they were lines of poetry. Outside Papi's car, there's a German shepherd posing in the backseat of a Volvo and one of Papi's girlfriends hitch-hiking with her thumb out. We hasten to run her over and I keep track of all the run-over girlfriends with chalk marks on the glove compartment. Dogs and girlfriends, pedigreed dogs and girlfriends. Chow chows, poodles, and Siberian huskies shake their manes against the wind like the models on those ads for Oriental fans.

Let me explain something to you, Papi says; he's always explaining something to me. We've been on the run for a while. And it's been some time since Papi and I have seen anybody other than me and him and him and me. And sometimes those dogs and girlfriends. I make faces at Papi from the backseat through the rearview mirror (when we're not face to face) as we zoom along in his Mercedes, eating Cheetos, Snickers, and gummy bears that leap from my hand and die under the seat. We also sleep in the Mercedes, which is champagne colored and has electric windows and a little bell that rings to tell us to put on our seat belts. But we never wear them and the bell eventually gives up. I love how the Mercedes smells inside and I poke my fingers into the beige leather to see how it changes under my nails. It's been a while since I cut them; Papi cleans them with a little knife that has a golden Christ on the handle with emeralds on the crown of thorns.

When night falls, or when Papi gets tired of driving, we stop at one of the parking lots for people like us on either side of the highway and throw the seats back. Sometimes Papi sleeps, but I can't sleep and so I push the door open and walk to the edge of the highway and wave at the other cars that go by or mentally count the red ones, blue ones, gray ones. One time I wanted to cross and stood there with one foot on the sidewalk and one on the highway so I could feel the vibrations of the trucks and cars passing so quickly before my eyes, until my own sandaled foot on the asphalt started to look like some other girl's foot, like a foot in a photo, and I got scared and went back to the car and pretended to sleep.

Let me explain something to you, Papi says to me. We're going very fast on the autopsy. The freeway! Papi corrects me: The freeway! Every ten kilometers there's one of these, Papi says as he sticks his entire arm out the window as if he's gonna shake the ash from a cigarette, but instead he points to some buildings in the shape of Hershey's Kisses, like Aladdin's palaces, or a sultan's, or a genie's, or where a flying carpet might come out. That's so people like us will slow down, Papi explains, cuz the buildings are a sign of those cafeterias we see every so often. They offer breakfast and sodas and quarter liter cartons of milk, which we first give to a kitten or a stray dog to make sure Papi's girlfriends aren't trying to poison us. What Papi complains about are the scrambled eggs. He always says what we ate at the previous cafeteria was better and so I imagine that, every ten kilometers or so, the eggs just get worse and worse until infinity in the direction Papi and I are traveling, while in the opposite direction they get better and better, win contests, and receive presidential honors. But then Papi interrupts me with a hot dog and a 7 Up, or an ice-cream bar that drips down his hand and we take off again.

Papi puts on a cassette with a song we both like a lot: a boy says he's lost his Unicorn brand jeans, to look for them, please, but the boy doesn't say, I've lost my Unicorn brand jeans, but yesterday I lost my blue unicorn, and so you think the boy is talking about a unicorn and not about his jeans. Papi explained this to me. He said: The thing is, some places make scrambled eggs in the microwave, that's why they're so bad. Later he explains how the microwave works and how a soldier with a firearm had a corn kernel in his pocket and it turned into popcorn and that's how the microwave and the bad eggs came about. Let me explain this to you: There are rays you don't see, but if they hit your hand, they'll give you cancer.

Sometimes Papi gets lost and we go into these little towns for hours at a time. Papi gets out of the car and makes calls from telephone booths. I lower the window and rest my elbow on the edge, singing, chewing gum, and cracking my knuckles. Papi tells me to be quiet as he covers his ears like a singer and hits the phone with the receiver in his hand and then spits and kicks the phone saying, Goddammit, goddammit, son of a bitch.

It's been a while since the only thing Papi and I see are dead skunks, rocks, landscapes, the lights on the highway, microwaveable breakfasts and dinners, people who serve popcorn directly out of their pockets to people like us who, for the most part, are not tourists but truck drivers. I wonder if they're all going to the same place we are. Sometimes Papi makes a call or meets somebody in a dark parking lot while I stay in the Mercedes listening to a baseball game in English and the only thing I understand is the applause. Sometimes Papi leaves the highway and we see little stores, little streets, closed barbershops, and not one living soul cuz it is very late, it's about four in the morning. We stop in a supermarket parking lot and Papi tells me not to worry, but I wasn't worried. Later, an Impala and a Lincoln go by and a wine-colored Cadillac parks close to us and Papi gets out of our car and walks towards the Cadillac, where there is a fat man with a mustache and a very black shock of hair. He wears a gray Polo shirt with a black neckline and a gold watch. Papi opens the Mercedes's trunk to show the fat man the things we've bought along the way, saying, Let me explain this to you. He demonstrates the Nikon by taking a photo, the tennis racket by fanning a forearm in the air, and the cassette player he bought me by playing a cassette by Billy Idol; he even lets him listen to a little piece of "Dancing with Myself." It makes me wanna show the fat man the Transformers watch Papi bought me that afternoon and so I open the door and raise my doll to show the fat man my watch, but the fat man is on the ground while Papi tries to wake him up with a kick to the head as he cleans his pistol with a little Donald Duck towel, which was the last thing we bought.

Close the trunk, Papi tells me as he throws the fat man

over his shoulder to take him back to his Cadillac. But since he's holding the pistol in his mouth I don't understand him too well when he says something that I think is not to worry, but I wasn't worried. We're the only ones in this parking lot, which is huge, just the fat man's Cadillac and the Mercedes and a line of supermarket carts that fit together like Legos. I check the time on my Transformers watch as Papi explains: He's just sick. He sits the fat man at the wheel of his Cadillac, puts the pistol in his hand, gives him a little kiss on the forehead, and shuts the door.

One day we finally stop at a motel with a pool but Papi doesn't let me get in it, so I turn the TV volume all the way up so I won't hear everybody else splashing about. We're finally in Orlando, Papi tells me as he squeezes a blackhead on his chin in front of the mirror. I nod, the remote control in my hand. Later, Papi opens a map and stretches it out on the bed to explain that Epcot Center is right here. He uses his finger to circle something on the map and then underscores the word *Orlando* with the same finger on the map and I understand. The center of the universe. Then Papi says, I'll be right back. Don't open the door for anybody, understand? He's wearing a Dodgers cap cuz the Dodgers' manager is Manny Mota. For a while I'm fine watching videos on MTV so I can tell somebody about them later. Later, I understand Papi is never coming back and that's why he left the map on the bed. I grab the corner of the map and pull it towards me and the paper crunches and cracks like little exploding firecrackers. I try to fold it back into its original rectangle shape and it sounds like more firecrackers. Papi has stopped at a gas station and he's forgetting about me, he's fueling up and forgetting about me. I'm gonna stay here in Orlando, living forever in this room with the volume on the TV all the way up, watching MTV, never opening the door for anybody, memorizing each scene in the videos so I can tell somebody about them someday, with a badly folded map and never visiting Epcot Center.

But Papi always comes back. Sometimes I'm sleeping when Papi shows up and what wakes me is the smell of hamburgers and the warm paper they come wrapped in. Papi and I eat the hamburgers, cheeseburgers, bacon mushroom cheeseburgers. Papi makes his mouth like a hamburger and fixes the straw on a huge 7 Up and offers it to me with hamburger eyes. Later, I lay on my belly to watch TV and Papi rests his back on the headboard holding an apple pie in his mouth like a dog would a puppy, cuz both of his hands are busy, one with the remote and the other with one of my feet. Papi pulls on my toes to crack them and they pop and I throw a fit.

When Papi wakes me up to tell me we have to go, he says I talked in my sleep. I don't remember a thing. But he says it's true, that I spent the night talking in my sleep. It's cuz of the cartoons, Papi says. But I don't remember. When we go out to the parking lot, I tell Papi, Look at that, how pretty it is, and I'm signaling the switchblade sticking out of one of the tires on the Mercedes. Papi gets switchblades stuck in his tires all the time. I figure it's his girlfriends.

Then Papi tells me to get in the car and I get in the car, but I don't turn on the radio. He changes the tire, using his foot on the hydraulic jack to lift the car, and looking up and down at that switchblade with apple-pie eyes.

We drive for a long time and I don't dare ask about Epcot Center, not even when I see a big shiny ball with a little stairway up one side like a ship about to take off. Papi reads my mind and explains: Water. And now I know how this is all gonna end, all this Epcot Center, all this Mickey Mouse. In the end they take me to the Miami Seaquarium and let me push a little dolphin-shaped cart. We look at the dolphins and the whales as they jump in the pool and a girl sticks her head inside a whale but I'm still waiting for Mickey Mouse when I look at my Transformers watch, cuz Papi told me Mickey Mouse and Donald Duck were also coming to look at the dolphins.

seven

Papi goes so fast that whoever goes after him is always late. He goes so fast the only thing you see is the cloud of smoke he leaves behind. But I go faster than Papi, and when I hear his voice calling me from the parking lot to hurry up, I yell back that I just have to put on my shoes even though I'm still blinded by the shampoo and in the shower.

Papi's girlfriends are faster than everybody and they've set up an office to organize themselves so they can coordinate their dates with Papi. They now have their own secretary who communicates with Papi's secretary (cuz secretaries understand each other best) and they're all beautiful and there are so many of them (both secretaries and girlfriends) that they sometimes have to rent out a hotel to get to know each other and trade business cards, which, besides the girlfriend's name, profession, and telephone number, also shows her turn on the long list of dates with Papi. The list is so long they soon have to update the system, computerize it, and bring in foreign technicians to offer training for the girlfriends so they'll be ready when the new system is activated.

Of course, Papi pays for everything.

The media soon finds out about the updates being made to the installation. It's first on a long list of steps to modernize the system, say two foreign technicians in the newspaper photo who look like they could be Colombian or German, or twins with fake mustaches. The day finally arrives and the system is activated in a glamorous reception at which Papi and his girlfriend of the day cut a ribbon (with Papi's colors) for the cameras. In the meantime somebody opens a bottle of champagne but all we can see is the crest of foam. After the photo is taken, the girlfriend of the day cedes the spotlight to the next girlfriend, who is currently sitting in the makeup chair having her cheekbones retouched. The people at home, the guests and the girlfriends themselves, confirm the system's high efficiency. For three days, a radio and television network transmits news bulletins every half hour that explain the enrollment process, the correct way to fill out the application, how to present yourself to the right offices to solicit the list of necessary documents, and the deadline for turning them in. Between news bulletins they show movies starring Joselito, Marisol, or *Marcelino, pan y vino*.

We've lost sight of Papi. There's no cloud of smoke or anything. There are just photos from three or four years ago that pop up now and again in the newspaper when his name is mentioned in some mix-up, always cuz of one of his damned girlfriends.

By the time the technicians realized the system wasn't programmed according to the country's protocols for electricity (rushed and scarce), it was already too late. With each blackout the system began to weaken and the small delays began to create a curtain of residual time behind which Papi could hide and disappear, which he did for months at a time. Poor guy, he was just so tired.

Finally a group of women whose turn had been denied various times got together and renounced the system, saying it was fraudulent and demanding an open and immediate meeting with Papi, and the dismissal of the central committee (which had, until now, been in charge of the administration and maintenance of the internal and external structure of the system). They questioned Papi's very existence, that of the system, and of the list itself.

But nobody could find Papi. The women recited manifestos from their own radio network, demanding direct contact, a more equitable agreement, and lined up in front of Papi's office. The line grew very quickly, reaching Calle 27 de Febrero just minutes before the first woman got to the door. In an hour the line reached Avenida Kennedy and the next day it was in the dead zone between the capital and the nearby provinces.

There were too many women. I think some didn't even know what they were doing there. Some just happened to be passing by with their husbands, walking their dog or in a car, and without even saying good-bye, they threw themselves from the moving vehicles, got in line, and were immediately absorbed into the conversation about how nail strengthener is made from a garlic base.

The line continues to grow, attracting those giant flies that follow the vendors with their roasted peanuts, boiled corn, fried plantains, tripe, bofe, mofongo, hot dogs, pork sandwiches, rice and beans, coconut sweets, tamarind juice, frío-fríos, yun-yuns, and little empanadas. Some are quite clever and park their pickup trucks every two blocks loaded with T-shirts, posters, caps, scapulars, and all kinds of propaganda featuring Papi's photo. Some even have photocopies of Papi's birth certificate and green card, framed in fake gold, with the Virgin of Altagracia in the center. Some of the women come up and buy and the merchandise looks great on them, but others come up carrying scissors and lighters to put the buyers on trial cuz, after all, *What are we doing here?*

The merchants have their own line parallel to that of the women. They see this could be good business so they set up a little stand made of sticks and plywood. Soon there's a long line of stands that extends to the mountain range on either side of the river of people.

At night those who can sleep hug one another or a stuffed animal and lie down on cardboard and mats, protected by the two lines of stands, carts, and posts that the peddlers cover with a tarp or sky-blue plastic when they go home. There's always one vendor who stays twenty-four hours to offer coffee, Guardia mints, and bananas to those who suffer from insomnia. They gather around a battery-operated fan somebody has managed to get, or around a little television to see if anybody has seen Papi, or to see how the line is doing, or to see Papi in those photos from three years ago that sometimes show up on the news whenever his name is mentioned in some mix-up. A union organizer pleads for a place in line so he and Papi can meet and discuss the state of things: the line itself, its extension, the women who won't even listen to God and interfere with traffic at certain hours, who bite each other, who tear each other's nails cuz somebody cut in front of them, who fall on the asphalt and break their necks and need an ambulance to pick them up and take them straight to Papi.

Some of the women are pregnant. Since no one will make them leave the line and lose their turns while getting a checkup, the government has brought in various mobile gynecological clinics to dispense prenatal vitamins, creams to eliminate stretch marks, and free exams during daylight hours. The mobile clinics are even equipped with ultrasounds so the mothers can see how their babies are developing, and in general, it's true that they look like Papi. The pregnant women are given priority in line, which means the others, seeing their own position imperiled, make them miscarry by putting two Situtex in their breakfast. And if that doesn't work, they grab them and take them behind a tree and use a hanger. Many bleed to death in the ditches. It's very ugly.

When the survivors first began to give birth, they brought the babies to my abuela Cilí, believing she'd intervene with my father. But Cilí is very old and really can't deal with any of that, so I answered the phone like a secretary and organized the appointments. To those I didn't like over the phone, or who didn't recognize me right away, I'd say, Yes, yes, this Sunday at such-and-such an hour, and when they arrived I'd say I didn't see their names in the book and they'd have to leave. Later I'd see them going down the stairs with their rag-doll baby drooling milk and I'd feel sorry for them and say, Wait, wait, I think I can find you a slot, and I'd run my hand over the pages of the book and lick the tip of my index finger with my tongue to turn the page.

Cilí bathes early. She wears a dress that makes her look like she's kind of in mourning and pulls out the plastic bag in which she keeps our money in moist wads; I don't know if it's sweat or water or what. She gives me five pesos and says, Buy yourself a soda. I go down the stairs and buy a pack of Constanza cigarettes and go up to the roof and stick one in my mouth but I don't light it, instead pretending to blow smoke through my nose the way Milly taught me. That's when Cilí calls me cuz the mothers have started to arrive. Leysi offers them coffee on the stairway and carries the little kids around and cries and hugs each one of the mothers cuz Tía Leysi loves a scene. When she comes back in the house she pulls the curtain shut and says, What a bunch of sluts!

My abuela sits the babies on her lap and, smiling, checks their ears, checks their toes, and their penises with a magnifying glass. She looks for a little birthmark in the form of a crab that might match Papi's. Some of the babies have two birthmarks, one in the form of a crab and the other shaped like a pipe, just like the one on Papi's dad's dad. Some of the kids look exactly like me, and in fact there is a long line of women with kids wearing knitted wool socks or miniature Nike-brand shoes who look exactly like me; it extends from Cilí's door all the way to the Malecón. At some point they realize Cilí isn't gonna get them a car, or a meeting with Papi, or monthly support, and they go back to the line at the dealership, with their kids and all, many of them already grown.

eight

Your adventure awaits but first you have to understand the backstory. Solid knowledge of the backstory before starting the game will make the adventure much richer. It's important to know the relationship between Papi, his business associates, the family, and the Lord of All Darkness, also known as his girlfriends.

Up there, where the devil lost his sandal, that is, in the middle of fucking nowhere, that's where Papi is enthroned. This mountain-castle-tower with a thousand stories is the source of all his suffering and happiness here on Earth and all adjacent worlds. Papi increases in power thanks to the energy given off by everyone in the world who wants a new car. Papi's powers bloom when the spirit of those who yearn vibrates at its highest, until they let their women go with the watchmen and sell their kids one by one just so they can buy a car at Papi's dealership, where they're given the magic key so they can fly, get women, and eventually more keys.

At the beginning, his business associates were loyal to Papi and the foundational link between Papi and the lesser world, but then one day his associates united against him. But Papi knows everything and can do anything, so he escaped in time, and they're still looking for him. Since then, Papi's business associates manage Papi's empire. A doll dressed in one of Papi's suits, or one of his associates, the guy who looks most like Papi, the one who had a bit of surgery done, is who reigns in the mountain-castle-tower of a thousand stories. They keep people calm with images and prerecorded speeches from before Papi disappeared. In these videos, Papi never gets old, though his associates age and get ugly and richer and richer.

The girlfriends used to be loyal to Papi, but devotion has ruined their souls cuz Papi condemned them to forty years without dick. This consumes the girlfriends and they look for Papi everywhere, following all the fake dicks that his buddies have strewn all over the place.

The girlfriends who got off on these dicks now fall prey to another curse: sharks, shark imitators, pterodactyls that chase everybody so they can suck their necks for the last drop of Papi's blood left in those veins, roosting in the doorjambs, on the roofs, on antennas, and laying eggs in newspaper nests, while the rest of the world's population chases them away with buckets of Astringosol and boiling water.

Papi's children all look the same, albinos with ash-colored hair and blue eyes, and they all wear little sailor outfits. They don't always come out of pterodactyl eggs. Sometimes they're born in dumpsters through spontaneous generation. They crawl into a single file and go door to door looking for Papi, asking for a helping hand.

When Papi's business associates saw how the children multiplied, they decided to adopt as many as they could and gave them names like Xavi, Hansel, Guille, Axel, and sent them to American schools where they had lockers and got a sexual education. The rest of Papi's children fell into two groups: those who stayed in line with their mothers, and those who renounced Papi and their mothers and dyed their hair some other color, even though you can always recognize them by their white roots.

Then there's the royal family, which is me, my abuela, my aunts, and the twins, Puchy and Milly. There's also my mother, recognized by Papi's royal family as Papi's only wife cuz she was the first and they married the way God intended, in the church. The family is in charge of the safekeeping of Papi's attributes. They're also in charge of revealing his mysteries to me at the right time if they see I have the potential to take on this adventure. The twins are considered part of the family and must look out for me and Papi's attributes.

One other thing: sometimes these creatures, monsters and heroes both, don't look the part, and they get mixed up cuz they act as if nothing is going on. Some don't even realize they are pterodactyls or business associates or part of the royal family. To identify who's who, we've installed a radar right in this text that sends a signal that reads and classifies everyone on a screen for those still walking and talking. This radar is the only thing with which we initiate our conferences.

The principle objectives are to intercept and interrupt the business associates' evil industry and to find Papi, which would restore order and peace in the world. To reach these objectives we must first overcome numerous obstacles. The lots at the mall, elevators, roofs, beauty salons, town squares, the caves, the resorts, and everywhere else, all booby-trapped, all crawling with monsters. We must conquer them step by step, word by word. Enemies won't be the only thing we will meet along the way. There will also be friends to help and give a hand. Listen closely to what they have to say.

1. Gather Information

Whenever you encounter others, stop and listen (see page X). Use the information to determine which path to take. Whenever you meet with someone, you should know where to go from there. Be sure to chat with everyone. The person you shun might turn out to be the one with the clue to victory (no one will teach you the strategies, you'll have to figure them out on your own).

2. Fight with Enemies

The devil's on the loose and there are monsters everywhere. You'll gain the experience you need to deal with them and survive. But as the adventure proceeds, the monsters multiply (or grow more deadly). With each monster you eliminate, you'll get stronger. Don't give up on these battles.

THE WORLD

The world is divided into three areas: the street, the home, and everything else. This last may include the countryside, the sky, the bottom of the sea, TV, space (different from the sky), the mountain-castle-tower with one thousand stories, the beach, the Internet, terraces, music, airports, stores, and temples.

1. The Street

This is the outside world. Monsters lurk here. We'll discuss neighborhood types later. The street is the richest source of information, not just via people, but also via signs, graffiti, flyers.

2. Home

This includes all furnishings, car and airplane interiors, jail cells and hideouts, underground tunnels, public bathrooms, laundromats, cafeterias, restaurants, hospitals, and hotels. Generally speaking, monsters don't invade the home and when they do, they're chief monsters in disguise. Homes are riddled with traps, loose ends, abysses, cul-de-sacs, and secret passageways.

3. Everything Else

Many people live in these places. People and monsters. But monsters don't do much here, and people just do their thing. This is where you must find the objects necessary for victory. To recharge: in case of injury, rest. This is how the best-quality information comes about, and disseminated every which way, it can be perceived by all the senses.

SPECIAL FEATURES

Jigsaw puzzles (see page X)

These are usually found at home, in rooms with a switch. When the switch is turned on, it usually reveals a secret stairway or something like that.

Shortcut (see page X)

Some of the walls in the house are weak and hollow and can be torn down with the help of something like a spoon. Later there will be instructions about which item to use in these cases.

Weapons (see page X)

Some weapons have uses other than attacking enemies. A fork, for example, can help you make your way through the cabin of a plane you've just hijacked but it can also bring nourishment to your mouth.

ATTACKS

Since monsters are everywhere, attack them with weapons, with items and magic. Speed is the key to victory. There are many weapons and they're all very effective, especially pistols, but each monster is vulnerable to a different weapon. I like pistols best. Oh, and axes.

SPELLS

SLEEP: This means yawning, which will cause all the other monsters to do the same, and will give you the opportunity to toss a grenade in their mouths.

SLEEP 2: To pretend to be sleeping (see page X).

MUTE: This spell causes monsters to fall silent, leaving only their lips moving.

FIRE: Light any accessible flammable material (curtains are recommended) with a lighter and, best-case scenario, the enemy's hair (if the enemy has hair).

ICE: Ignore the monsters, pretend to be cool.

nine

The line grows longer and wider. Every hour, young and old women join in, bringing along their children, their neighbors, their things. The line grows so long, it comes all the way here and I tell Mami I think we should get in before it's too late. She says that's not necessary. She doesn't realize people give her strange looks when she says I'm Papi's daughter. People look at her and think she's a fool who believes she's part of the royal family. Sometimes I think so too. I mean, the day Charles and Lady Di's wedding was broadcast, I was sure Diana was my mom, my real mom, and that she'd come get me in a carriage.

   I climb up on the building's roof to see if Diana, still wearing her wedding dress, is on her way. I wanna see if her carriage is entering the parking lot and coming to get me and to tell ¡Hola! magazine I'm her real daughter and she's my real mother. But the only thing I can see down there are the balls of so many heads in line. From up here, I spit a green phlegm that inevitably hits a blonde with a perm in the eye. The line is so thick it's impossible to tell which way it's going. Could be forward or back or to the sides. What you see on the street is just a mob of people talking, holding little plastic bags full of plantain chips or corn on the cob, the ditches filling with glasses of foam just like the lines to get into Quisqueya Stadium for a baseball game.

There are huts everywhere, trucks carrying construction materials, Titan Concrete logos on the sides of those steel hulks. Cranes and more cranes turning their brontosaurus heads, kilometric cranes that gulp down mouthfuls of sand at the beach and drop them in little piles to bury people on the shore, though sometimes they also drop them in the right places at construction sites. The only things you can see now are heads and construction materials. Colored blocks one on top of the other, mimicking the wall where they'll be placed, one on top of the other every which way. Glass for windows, frames for doors, wooden, metal, and plywood doors. Rods for towers, rods for multifamily units, rods for apartment complexes, nails, screws, wooden blocks, hinges, baseboards, PVC, kilometers of wire, and door handles. Rods for schools, for churches, for hospitals, rods leaning, rods in the sun, reddish rods, rods taking a nap.

What you see now are craters, holes bigger than the devil, cuz the higher the tower, the bigger the hole, and the line starts to break and fall into the depths of this abyss. Down there, a bulldozer gathers the bodies and places them next to the rocks and roots the same bulldozer pulled out earlier in the afternoon. The dirt in the holes is orange, red, and the sun strikes the red-dirt balls and crags. The bulldozers are yellow and driven by little Playmobil men whose faces are never seen.

New towers appear every day on the streets, toward the end of the line. At night, trucks unload materials for reinforced concrete, sometimes even on top of the people sleeping here. Then the people fall in the mix and become spontaneous sculptures; there's the scattered brains of someone who had a load land on their head, in spite of a rope and pulley. And everywhere, there are the bodies of Haitian workers impaled on straight rods cuz they toppled from the building's fourteenth floor. They throw themselves on purpose, the architects tell the newspaper. They throw themselves on purpose to see, if they live, if we will give them money.

When the projects are finished, the inaugurations are televised. They play a video of Papi from a kickoff years ago; I can always tell cuz whatever he's wearing has been out of fashion for years now. In front of each project there's a sign that says Papi Did This. I imagine one of Papi's associates' hands signing the checks.

But not all the projects are completed and so there are half apartments, half airports, half malls, half bridges with rods hanging like teeth and pointing at the bottom of the river. The city is now a mock-up on which thousands of pastel or phosphorescent painted two- and three-unit buildings are being raised, each unit with its own balcony, its own ferns and aloes and snake plants in brick-colored pots. Most of the landscape is taken over by the skeletons of houses, buildings, towers, and storefronts that, one budget cut ago, surrendered to creeping vines and a post-satanic cult that needed shelter.

The housing is distributed according to the results of urine tests that confirm a relationship to Papi, though the results can be tricked up by drinking Papi's blood or vinegar or by filling out a thirty-page questionnaire in which the applicant relates all manner of Papi anecdotes, including exact dates and places. In the meantime, there are photo studios and support centers getting rich off the illiterates who come to dictate their stories and have their 2 × 2 picture taken so they can attach it, as required, to the questionnaire. Some centers also clandestinely hand out Papi's blood—no one knows how they get it—and a few others (more sophisticated) give out little baby-food jars guaranteed to be filled with his urine.

Now there are also lines to confirm blood ties, lines to hand out keys (Tuesdays at 6 p.m.), lines to go into department stores with really good specials where, every now and then, a couple of ladies will start a fight over the last ceiling fan with bell-shaped bulbs. And everywhere—on billboards, at intersections, on electric signs, on the murals on those salty walls along the Malecón—there's Papi's face and the colors of the flag, and below him a slogan like a prayer: We're All Family.

My part of the family, the royal family, got an apartment in La Feria neighborhood when they were being handed out. It's a three-story building in front of the Lotería Nacional: we're in 3A. At the Lotería Nacional they raffle off a date with Papi every Sunday and then the rest of the week they keep people calm by giving away money, Jet Skis, and electric knives. Every day from nine to five you can hear two voices announcing prizes, one a man's, one a woman's. One voice calls out the winning number and the other responds with the prize, which is almost always six hundred and fifty pesos. And we (six hundred and fifty pesos!) are the privileged few (six hundred and fifty pesos!) who don't need (six hundred and fifty pesos!) a radio to hear them. The speakers (seven hundred and fifty pesos!) can be heard all over the block (six hundred and fifty pesos!) and shake the cups (six hundred and fifty pesos!) Cilí has in her china hutch (third prize!).

They've gotten me a little job (six hundred and fifty pesos!) at a flower shop (six hundred and fifty pesos!) which, they say, Papi set up for a country girl who lives in 2D (six hundred and fifty pesos!). I spend all day there spraying white flowers (six hundred and fifty pesos!) with an indigo spray (three thousand five hundred pesos!) while the woman answers the phone and says things like, We have gladiolus that can tell time (main prize!).

My pay at this job includes letting me paint the flowers, which I love, and hanging out in the AC, which the flowers need all day long. They also let me play with the little green bricks they use to keep the flowers standing in the arrangements. I don't know the name of the material these little bricks are made of but they always have to be wet, and so they keep them in a yellow plastic baby tub to which we add ice water now and again. I do this too. The owner told me one day she's gonna teach me to make ikebana and that you can earn a living making ikebana, that she knows a woman who supports five kids making ikebana, and I have to ask what the hell that means. The owner's son spends the entire day in a minivan delivering flowers, and when he comes back at night we have dinner together if Cilí hasn't called me. Sometimes they invite me to watch a horror movie with them. The other day they screened *Santo versus the She-Wolves*—she-wolves! The flowers are for births, weddings, lovers, and funerals, but we arrange more flowers for deaths than anything else.

La Feria neighborhood has several names. Some say its real name is Matahambre, or Hungerkiller, but others say Hungerkiller ends three streets away. When there's mail at Cilí's, which is almost always just postcards I sent when I visited Papi, I look at the address to see what they put and it almost always says Centro de Los Héroes. Puchy says it's called that cuz a lot of heroes died here but Milly throws a potato she's been peeling at him and says, Don't fill the girl's head with nonsense. Tía China, who knows more than the twins cuz she's been going to the Universidad Autónoma for about ten years, tells me the neighborhood's real name is Feria de la Confraternidad y el Mundo Unido—or, Fraternity and World Unity Market. She says that's the name Papi gave the neighborhood, and when Papi names something, nothing can change it. She says he bestowed this name cuz, about two blocks from Cilí's house, there's a monument in the shape of a little ball representing the earth and this monument is really the center of the world.

I've seen that little ball, which is just a cement globe. After four in the afternoon, just as the sun is going down, that's when the hos (that's what they call the whores) start hanging around. And after seven, when the sun is completely gone, queens and little fag glue sniffers begin to make their rounds, and then the cops with their billy clubs come to beat whomever doesn't go around the little earth ball six hundred and fifty times. There's also a bug-filled fountain that shoots water only on an occasional Sunday. It's surrounded by very tall poles from which, according to what Puchy tells me, there used to be flags from different countries. People would come by in their cars back when hardly anybody had a car, and they'd circle the fountain and wear white linen. That's when Milly throws a tube of toothpaste at Puchy's head.

It's a few steps from the little ball of the world to our building. The little ball is next to the Lotería Nacional, which is why the queens, the glue-sniffing fags with their jars of glue, and the whores practically live in our lot.

Night and day it's filled with white plastic chairs, with empty Presidente and Bohemia beer bottles scattered about the chair legs. People play dominoes and tell jokes as if they weren't in line, as if nothing were going on in the shade of those jabilla trees. They're leafy like almond trees, but their fruit, with a light green rind and a velvety down, is terribly poisonous.

On the first floor there's a Turk who claims to know Papi from the navy, and he established a grocery and fish market people used to complain about cuz they'd go in to buy a pound of rice or a quart of oil and come out reeking of fish. In the end, the grocery and fish market became just a grocery, cuz nobody likes fish that much anyway. Then the Turk, seeing all those people out in the lot, put up two towering speakers he kept going day and night, competing with the lottery prizes, and blasting all the merengue hits of the moment.

The drains around the building don't work and are full from the rains, the hurricanes, and the soapy excess from the women who do their laundry on the sidewalks. The water gets thick and green and nasty, a foamy sauce that practically requires a drawbridge to get over. One day I stuck a branch in but when I pulled it out, it was just a string of smoke; the green stew had consumed it like battery acid. I immediately rushed home and got a bottle of Coke so I could fill it with that thick goo and stick it under my bed. First, I showed it to Moise and Zequi (whose real names are Moisés and Ezequiel), two brothers who live in 1A, Pepe's kids, Leysi's best friend. They're evangelicals and so they don't have priests or nuns. People just come over, usually bearing biblical names. I wish I had a biblical name. I'd like to point to a section of the Bible with my name in it that says I did this or that. Zequi showed me his section and I was very impressed, that is, until Moisés showed me his.

Pepe (whose real name is Esperanza) is always buttering a piece of Pepín bread. She's almost always sitting with a bag of Pepín bread on her lap and a stick of butter in her hand. She takes a piece of bread and butters it and hands it to Zequi or Moise or their little brother Dundo, the youngest, who's pretty slow but knows Ecclesiastes from one end to the other and recites it as he plucks little turds from his butt with his thumbnail. All four are illuminated by a gas lamp cuz the transformer on the corner exploded this afternoon and the electric company still hasn't sent anyone to fix it. The lamplight hits Pepe's face, which is very dark, with very black eyes, with gray hairs only by her ears. The light also gleams on the metal cups Pepe uses to serve Tang to her kids before the brothers and sisters from church come over to sing and clap and play the tambourine, occupying all seven rocking chairs in Pepe's living room, rocking chairs on which on more than one occasion the Holy Spirit has rocked.

And almost always, between this and that psalm, between this and that song, the pastor speaks in tongues and he and some other brother twist their ankles all the way around like the girl turning her head in The Exorcist. There's a very slight mist that comes in off the street, a mix of pee and cigarette smoke.

That pee stink comes from Boque Sopa, a drunk who lives under the stairs and pisses everywhere. Boque Sopa (whose real name is Jesús) must be about thirty years old, but he looks older than Cilí. He's white but he wears an afro and his eyes are red all the time. When he first got here, everybody got together to get him little jobs. They said he could clean the ditches, they told him, or pick up empty beer bottles to sell, or trim the trees, or wash cars, or sweep and mop the stairs. There's so much you can do, they told him. The neighbors gave Boque Sopa a set of tools, a box for the tools, an orange hoodie with a stripe (phosphorescent, just like the firefighters), a hat, rubber boots, a rake, but Boque Sopa drank it all up that very night. Cuz Boque Sopa can drink anything. It's a miracle! shouts Boque Sopa when he wakes up naked on the flat cardboard where he sleeps and, once more, everything's vanished. With his eyes redder than the devil's, and with the gardening shears still in his hand (he slept gripping them), he climbs up to Cilí's to see if she'll give him one of the twins' jeans or a T-shirt of mine or a small bowl of soup, or whatever. Boque Sopa doesn't let go of those gardening shears anymore, though the jabilla trees in the park need more of an electric razor, but Boque Sopa makes the effort and hangs from a branch like a monkey, balancing the hand with the shears. The kids throw jabillas and rocks to knock him down. When he comes up asking for water with an empty Carnation milk can he rescued from the trash, Cilí, who's the only person who ever calls him by name, cuts a little piece of Camay soap to give him. Papi sends us soaps by the box, ditto with deodorants, detergent, and shampoo.

The cigarette smoke, however, doesn't come from Boque Sopa but from my tía Leysi, who won't go into Pepe's apartment when the brothers and sisters from the church are over smacking their palms in the name of Jesus Christ. Tía Leysi stays just outside the threshold of Pepe's door, where the hallelujahs get lost in the "one more, one more night, one more" coming from the speakers at the Turk's.

As soon as the brothers and sisters from church leave,

Tía Leysi goes in Pepe's apartment and Pepe sends out for the first three beers, which they down right there, their rockers going, back and forth and back and forth, until Leysi—the phone in her lap—starts dialing numbers real fast without breaking her long and purple nails and then, with the phone between her shoulder and chin, she proceeds to tell whomever answers that their daughters, sisters, granddaughters, or wives are a bunch of sluts, prostitutes, dykes, and bad seeds. While she's talking Leysi pokes a finger through the circle she's made with the thumb and index finger of her other hand. Then, relaxed, she and Pepe take the rockers outside, where someone immediately offers them their next beers, and Moise, Zequi, and I play vitilla in the parking lot, which is pretty much just playing baseball, except that instead of a bat and ball we use a stick and a water-bottle cap.

I saw when Tía Leysi, who'd just said somebody was a bastard, a cocksucker, and a dyke, rested her head on the back of her rocker and felt the blow. I saw the blow. I felt it too. I saw Boque Sopa come out of the shadows with his cap on backwards as if he were gonna ask if someone could just pour a couple of fingers' worth of beer in his Carnation can. He lifted the open shears and hit the back of the rocker where Leysi's head had been resting with one of the blades.

And Leysi—in her bubblegum stretch pants, and her shiny pink-sequin strapless blouse, her thick socks with pom-pom balls at the ankle, her white patent-leather heels, her fake gold rings, the naughtiest mouth in the neighborhood, and a braid of hair that's been bleached, ironed, colored, dried, and colored again a thousand times, and which was now a shade that could have passed for blond in a black-and-white movie—felt the blow of Boque Sopa's shears reflecting the light of the lamp-post on Avenida Independencia as they fell right smack between her braid and her head, cutting the long tail of hair from her scalp where it originated and the mocha-colored braid curled like a lizard's tail in a parking lot, and Tía Leysi in her rocker immediately cringed while the braid took off like a carnival rocket hurling towards the drunks who don't get out of the way in time, hitting their cheeks, ripping off their ears and fingers, and crashing into chairs, headlights, and spilled foam. Leysi begins to melt and her bubblegum Lycras melt with her, and her sequin strapless blouse (which we call baja-y-mama) also melts with her, until all that's left of Leysi on the rocker is a puddle that looks like pistachio ice-cream barf while a new Leysi has grown from the braid, this one wearing a skirt that reaches her ankles, a blouse with sleeves to her wrists, and a pair of black loafers. She carries a little packet of pamphlets about the end of the world, and her Bible.

At Cilí's house there are so many people the toilet pa-per only lasts about fifteen minutes, and then a hand emerges from the bathroom door, followed by a real stink of shit, asking for another roll. People come from every-where, in buses and on trucks, to get a visa, an apart-ment, a meeting with Papi, and sometimes they stay at Cilí's indefinitely. Milly makes pillows and cushions with the remnants of a mat someone gave her. She spends all her time on the roof cutting up the mat into smaller and smaller pieces, filling up fabric bags under the sizzling sun. Later, she tests them with her own head, putting the cushions down on the floor of the roof at high noon and falling asleep. I have to go wake her up so she won't burn to a crisp. Ever since Puchy got a visa and she didn't, the only thing Milly will do is go down to the grocery, buy herself a packet of Constanzas, and smoke them one by one while she cuts up the mat. Sometimes I help her. I also help her clean the house cuz Leysi is at church praying for a brother who's suffering from Alzheimer's and China is at the border. Cilí makes sure we're all fed, even though there's about ten thousand of us and new people just keep coming, saying, Hey, they're family, and they tell stories about Vale Juanchi or Vale Apolinai. But Cilí herself doesn't know who the hell they're talking about.

Cilí's spoon has a way of scooping out exactly the same amount from the pot for everyone. It doesn't matter how the spoon goes in, everyone gets the same amount of rice and pigeon peas, chicken in wine sauce, green plantains, and then, on top of the plantains, chicken sauce. The only person who gets less is Leysi, cuz she has bleeding ulcers and can only rarely get anything down. Leysi looks skinnier all the time in that huge skirt that's like a cape. In the morning when she opens her eyes, and even before she brushes her teeth, she grabs her Bible and, using a Paper Mate pen, jots down on a piece of paper the revelations she had during the night. What I see is a skeleton picking up the pen and writing.

The portion that Cilí doesn't serve Leysi she gives to China, or more precisely, she saves it in the fridge for whenever China wants it. When Tía Leysi sees the food covered with a second plate in the fridge, she says, Lucifer! Apparently, he lives with us as well. But it's just that there are so many of us, no one knows who's who. That's without counting the twenty or so additional souls who live in China and eat like crazy; they stick their heads out and talk through China while you're eating, asking if they can have the steak on your plate. It infuriates me.

Cilí told me we have to give it to them cuz we can't act with ill will towards the spirits, that these are beings in China and they walk around inside her as if they were on a bus or elevator. That's why I eat my steak before I even get to the table, cuz riding a skateboard on an empty stomach is very dangerous and the first thing I do after eating is go to the corner and wait for the other kids, for Soti, for Danny-p, and Batichica, who come with one foot on their skates and the other rowing like an oar. They grab on to the back of the bus and I join them going up Calle Churchill, sucking up all that black smoke the bus farts out its ass, until the driver realizes we're there and stops the bus. Another driver has let him know we're back there, and when he gets off the bus he's carrying a machete to use on us as if we were leeches, but we've already hooked on to another bus or a truck or a van that will take us to World on Wheels.

Besides the skate park, at World on Wheels there's a skating rink where there are frequent birthday parties. The guest tickets have three square stickers, one says beverage and two say pizza and these are equivalent to three beverages and two pizzas or two ice creams if the birthday kid's mom bought the right package. We don't get anything cuz we're there for another reason but we steal a ticket from a kid in the bathroom or we beg the birthday kid's mom to please get us a ticket in exchange for a photo with the birthday kid and the first person injured at the skate park.

Soti, Batichica, and the others get in line at the skate park and go down the ramp one by one, reflecting on the use of safety helmets as they drop headfirst into the cement. I position myself with my skateboard at the end of the line but I cede my turn to whomever comes up, extending my arm and saying, You first, After you. Some of them say: Hey you, lend me your deck and I lend it to them so they can lose some teeth while I stay at the end of the line. Some go down five or six times before I finally step out of line.

Soti and Batichica aren't friends of mine at all, and neither is Oche, or Danny-p, but I wait for them behind the jabilla tree at Independencia and Churchill until they show up, pushing their skateboards with one leg and drying their sweat with a Minor Threat or Dead Kennedys T-shirt. They grab on to buses and trucks and leap over walls, stairs, and slide on their tips down the handrails of the new metros, leaping around the building abandoned by Dominicana de Aviación until a watchman takes a shot at them.

I didn't get it. No matter how much I tried, I didn't get it. And then one day, Soti told me: Keep it loose, girl-friend, loose. But I didn't understand. Then one day I was riding on the edge of a little wall in a mall parking lot and I pushed the back end of the skateboard with my foot and bent forward in midair and I finally opened my fists and my fingers turned to spaghetti, noodles, a fork spiking spaghetti, *zazzz*. What I like most is the sound of broken bones when the skateboard lands and all those wheels drop and the trucks and then the sound of all those wheels going round a million miles an hour when we grab on to a bus en route to Bandera Plaza. Sometimes there's five of us in back and six to seven on each side hanging like oars off that bus, talking a million miles an hour with a million things going on in our heads. Then the mob in the bus pounds our fingers with rocks and hammers so we'll let go of the windowsills. But sometimes they give us friqui-taquis and quipes, as if we were African animals too close to the jeep during a safari. In this way you can see how many people fit in a bus, inside and out and even underneath, like in the movies, when they hang on to the axel with their teeth.

Around the corner, almost at Cilí's house, it's almost dark and some little girls sitting on a stoop shout at me: You with the long hair, you with the long hair, are you a girl or what? I turn around and lift my skateboard to smash their heads but the girls take off, their flip-flops flip-flopping up the stairs. In the dark I scream out all the skateboard tricks I don't know how to do yet (noseslide, three-sixty kickflips . . .), and as I say each trick I get bigger and bigger and bigger, until I can look in the window on the fourth floor, which is where those jerks live. They've hidden themselves under the bed but I stick my hand in through the window and with one quick knuckle sandwich I decapitate the little jerks' mom. I pull them out of their hideout and eat their bed and then I eat them, quickly, before China gets here.

Cilí told me that maybe I had the spirit too so I concentrated really hard to see if that was the case but it just made my head hurt. The spirits come over China now and again, and sometimes, at dawn, we have to get up to laugh at their jokes; sometimes there's more than one.

If a spirit has escaped from inside China, then you see her making faces, shaking her head, drooling, eating her own shit, hanging over the balcony half-dressed. The people who loiter out in the parking lot look up and say, Don't do it, don't do it. Then they open a sheet like a net, moving left and right depending on China's signals. When Boque Sopa sighs and says, Man, those spirits sure are mean, then the spirits leave China's body and run to the transformer on the corner, which explodes and splits the lamppost in two.

If the spirits are inside China, then you can see them chatting and drinking coffee in little paper cups and waiting until the elevator stops at the right floor. One day I even found Val Kilmer and Barry White and they thought they were on their way to the dentist, who apparently has an office in the same building. When the elevator opens, a spirit comes out and talks through China's voice. It looks, sniffs, holds on. But sometimes there are five or six of them at a time and so they divvy China up as much as they can: Changó speaks through her mouth; Ogún through her hands; Caonabo through her eyes and so on. When it's my turn I pretend I'm a spirit, Saint Santiago, the bull and Metresilí—I know them by heart—but the one I like most is Saint Santiago cuz, otherwise, when I'm being Caonabo, I have to drink liters of a golden cream punch Cilí offers me and which Caonabo and China love.

I have China in me all the time, especially when my fingers turn to spaghetti while I'm doing skateboarding tricks. From the moment I hit the back of the skate and bend in the air and my fingers turn into *zazzz*, I disappear, I turn into a cloud, I leave my body, and when I land the kids congratulate me cuz I just slid down a five-meter handrail and jumped twelve steps but the only thing I can remember is that I opened my eyes and I was at Cilí's house and Cilí was squeezing my feet (my tía China's feet) and saying: Who lives? When I spoke, it was in the voice of Caonabo, which is my voice mixed with China's voice, and Cilí was asking about the family and I responded and then, since there was no punch left, she brought me a little glass of rum I drank as best I could. I take advantage of the situation and tell her she has to give me more money, that this little girl deserves it.

When I go home without a scratch on me, Cilí pulls me aside and opens her closet, the one with the door that has a Juan Marichal baseball card tacked on it and a photo of Papi. Stick your hand in there, she says, and I stick my arm in a hole in the ceiling and pull out a bag I hand to Cilí. She extracts a wad of bills and gives me one, two, three hundred pesos. The next day at about seven in the morning I'm waiting for the skateboard shop to open so I can buy a Slayer T-shirt featuring a Nazi helmet with a vampire skull over an inverted pentagram and, below, the tour dates in bloody letters against a black background. What I like most is to hang out with Soti and the kids. It's not riding my skateboard, not at all, what I like most is hanging out wearing our black Metallica, Iron Maiden, and Sepultura T-shirts with sweat dried in whitish stains on the back and armpits. I wear my hair long so it'll cover my eyes and the only thing you can see is my mouth, which I twist, so when people see us they say: satanists, shit stinkers, and throw lemons and sour milk cartons at us and sometime even rocks but we don't say anything, with our T-shirts and twisted mouths, walking together with our skateboards in hand. Sometimes we throw back the rocks and lemons but we never hit them cuz they've already fled back to their homes.

One day Cilí wakes me up and says: Your dad, your dad. I run to the phone at Cilí's house, which is one of those ancient heavy black things, but Cilí pulls on my wrists and points to China, who's sitting in the dining room with her hand between her legs like Papi. I ask myself where this is gonna go. There's Papi with his long black hair, tits like melons, leather sandals, a silver ring on his little finger.

I play with his curls and say, Papi, how you've changed. Then Papi, in a voice that could be Caonabo mixed with China, Saint Michael mixed with Val Kilmer, the voice of Ozzy Osborne in Spanish, says: Comb your hair. That very night Huchi Lora, the most famous rhymer in the country, is on TV saying he has proof there's a narco-satanic cult operating in the Dominican Republic, trafficking in virgin blood, devouring fetuses, fist fucking, taking drugs, making human sacrifices, and that to identify those involved all you had to do was look at their T-shirts. That's when the cameras at Color Visión's Studio B do a close-up on an Ozzy record cover and Ozzy, like always, has a mouth full of blood.

Huchi had other evidence: record covers by Judas Priest, Megadeth, and Bob Marley with a marijuana leaf. The camera immediately scoured the criminal body and Freddy Beras-Goico, the host, took live calls from specialists (the head of the civil defensive, Doña Chucha, the spider clown) who recommended prayer and immediate intervention by the authorities. I covered up from head to toe, imagining groups of robed beings stealing babies from hospitals so they can make meat and plantain sandwiches, thinking about Ozzy and the taste of the fake blood he uses in the photos, about pig blood and blood in general. I didn't sleep a wink. Before the sun was up, I heard them coming up the stairs, the crashing of broken doors, the fucking chaos of their lasers cutting through the darkness in my room. I didn't understand a thing. They took me from the bed and lit my face with their lasers, then they illuminated my T-shirt and laughed and hit me on the head as they turned the house inside out. All you could hear was wood breaking and the glass shattering on Cilí's china cabinet. I screamed at Leysi: traitor, asshole, motherfucking bitch. She responded to the demon in me by hitting her head with a Bible, trembling with joy. Milly defended me from the black helmets as much she could but she could only do so much cuz they hit her with flashlights and lasers.

They shoved me, they cuffed me, they cut my hair right there and then, and they made me wear a yellow linen pleated skirt and blue patent-leather heels. Then they went on with their raid, which lasted forty days and forty nights of mattress tossing, closet emptying, breaking neck and clavicle bones under T-shirts, a poster, an Alpha Blondy keychain. If they find you on the streets wearing a black T-shirt—be it Mötley Crüe, the Misfits, or Sherwin-Williams—they confiscate it and throw you in jail for going shirtless in public. They cut your hair and give you a white T-shirt and buzz you right there with an electric razor so that on every corner and bus stop there are bunches of terrified kids wearing white T-shirts, their hair in clumps around their feet. And also piles of T-shirts, records, stripped cassettes, and posters on fire.

ten

The guy from Poison eats a whole box of Froot Loops before he goes on stage so he can get his dick up, so his dick will look bigger in that fuchsia Lycra when he's singing, his eyes made up and mouth painted as he grips the mic. The girls in the audience climb on each other's shoulders and lift their T-shirts and show off their little nips so they'll appear in the video and then stretch their arms like Elastic Man to grab his mic. The whole time he's singing, his makeup blending with sweat and the girls' spit and running all the way down to his dick, he's thinking about the beak on the Froot Loops toucan and he nods his head so hard his ropey hair swings back.

Juliana told me about this video before we even got out of the pool, before Rebeca's epileptic fit and the tangle of hair everyone saw peek from under her bathing suit when she started foaming at the mouth. I was scared. No one knew Rebeca was epileptic. Somebody said epileptics swallow their tongue and that scared me even more.

Juliana was telling me all about the Poison video, but we weren't talking about music or Poison but about dicks

cuz the swimming instructor had made all the boys practice the breaststroke. She'd sat her butt on the very edge
of a chair and she'd opened her legs and said, Like this,
like a frog. The boys would come one by one in their
little swimsuits to mimic the teacher and she'd fix their
legs then sit down and demonstrate again: Yes, yes, like
a frog. The boys would do it and you could see the bulges
on the side of their suits. You couldn't see anything on
the teacher cuz, while she'd tell them to practice kicking
in or out of the pool next to all the other kids from section 12 of Country Club Valenciano's summer camp, she
was almost always dry as a bone, wearing a sweat suit and
a stopwatch and holding a whistle between her teeth.

Juliana, who's also in section 12, doesn't swim very well,
and Rebeca doesn't matter, though she was also in section 12 and wore—like we all did—a T-shirt with the Country Club Valenciano logo, which is actually the Spanish
coat of arms, and a pair of blue shorts with white stripes
on the sides, like the kind we wear for gym at school.

The camp isn't a camp at all. There aren't any cabins
or campfires or pine trees or mountains. It's just a club
where our parents send us to play basketball so we won't
bug them at home. We play basketball, volleyball, tennis,
ping pong, karate, football, and Frisbee. Swimming is the
last class of the day and, sometimes, when it's cloudy, the
water's really cold.

First, with our heads out of the water: one two, one two.
Then the legs: one two, one two. Splashing water, kicking as if we really knew how to swim even though we're
holding on to the edge of the pool with both hands. Then
down, under the water, holding our breaths in big gulps
instead of in our lungs. I thought I'd never learn the butterfly. Even down below, you could hear the teacher's

voice, flat and dry, the whistle between her teeth, and her finger on the stopwatch counting down the time it takes me to get all shriveled up like a raisin.

When the teacher decides to get in the water, she takes off her sweatpants, folds them, and puts them on a chair. She takes off her hoodie and puts it on the back of the chair. She takes off her socks and then the last thing she takes off is the stopwatch, which she wears like a necklace. She puts it on her pants, makes her way to the edge of the pool, hopping and shaking her arms as she puts her very black and very short hair under a swim cap, then she snaps on her goggles. She quickly gets in position, launches herself and hangs in the air for about three hours before she slices into the chlorine water without causing the slightest ripple.

I love it.

When she finally pokes her head out, she's about halfway down the lap lane, doing the butterfly all the way to the other end, with that stunning back of hers that makes me wanna pee right there in the water, or to go crazy on everyone else and tell them to shut up and watch how she gets in and out of the water, the Speedo tag hanging off her suit.

Honestly, this is the class I like most.

When it's over, it's time to go but if we don't get picked up, then we just hang out in the pool. The club has three pools: the Olympic pool, the kids' pool, and the diving pool. The diving pool is the smallest and squarest but it's also the deepest. I once tried to touch the bottom but my ears almost exploded.

Just off the pool, there's a gazebo where guys hang out, their earphones plugged in, just watching the divers. Some guys are fully dressed but others take off their shirts so the girls can see their six-packs. Others undress down to their bathing suits and walk around the pool asking the sunbathing girls for their Hawaiian Tropic. Sometimes they dive in and perform tricks, jumping up and down on the diving board three or four times before diving in the water. Still others roll up into a fetuslike ball when they dive so they can soak the earphone-wearing guys who are watching. Sometimes one of the big guys, usually wearing a waterproof watch with a calculator, dives from the top board and does fifty-seven turns in the air only to land just outside the pool. The lifeguards rush to find his mouth so they can give him mouth-to-mouth but they can't find it, so a kid pulls the straw from his Coke bottle and the lifeguards stick it into the purée of blood and bones that's all that's left of the diver. They blow and the purée gurgles and they go on like this until the women from the infirmary show up with their menthol and a Band-Aid.

There's no camp on Saturdays, but there's a disco. They let me in cuz I'm very tall, which is why I'm in section 12 at camp with the girls who are already using tampons, although I really should be in section 10. The girls from section 12 are prepping a dance routine (with lambada skirts) to Miami Sound Machine's "Rhythm Is Gonna Get You" for the last day of camp. They don't let me take part cuz I don't have tits yet. That's what Juliana, the choreographer with two grapefruits on her chest, told me. She also said they were gonna wear color underwear under the lambada skirts so they could be seen when they did their turns.

Juliana dyes her hair, paints her fingernails, and French-kisses her boyfriends on the swings, meaning pretty much all the boys in section 14, and from section 15 on up. They grab her tits and I think they even suck on them. But nobody knows this. Just Juliana and her boyfriends, cuz Juliana doesn't talk about it with any of the other girls, just me, cuz I don't count, cuz I don't have tits. Juliana also knows a lot about the Bible and tells me the world is coming to an end and her mom said we have to have fun. That's why when we go to the disco on Saturday, she dances with the first guy who asks, which is almost always a fat blond boy with Z. Cavaricci pants and a Gap shirt. He squeezes her tight and licks her ear and corners her and then the only thing you can see of Juliana are her white heels up in the air and the blond boy's butt going up and down.

Juliana's not my friend or anything like that. She only talks to me when none of the other girls are around or when she wants to tell somebody what she did under the rainbow waterslide. Since I have a late pickup from camp and she does too, we sit on the swings and eat pizza or pierce my ears and then, as she holds ice to my earlobe to numb it, she tells me the monsters of the apocalypse are people and you have to be careful cuz they can turn you into a gargoyle on the spot. As she runs the needle with a green thread through my ear, she tells me we carry this stuff in our blood, that we carry our grandparents' and our great-grandparents' sins in our blood, and even the Tainos' sins cuz, though they were good people, they were godless. She also tells me there was a worker at the Coke factory who had AIDS and to take revenge on the world he cut his finger and threw it in one of the big containers. She knots the green thread so the piercing won't heal. Juliana also tells me that when she gets her period, she measures the oozing blood in millimeters. What a damned liar.

Since I don't get picked up sometimes, and neither does Juliana, we hide in the bushes by the swings and watch the people who come to have dinner at the club's piano bar. Some—always young people—come over by the swings and stick their hands in each other's pants and underwear and say, Oh yeah, oh yeah. Juliana loves this so she opens her Jem bag and takes out a pen and writes what people say on her hand.

One day Mami took me to the club but I didn't go in the disco. I just hung out in the parking lot, just looking at how pretty the empty tennis courts look when they're lit up. I let myself fall in the court's net and sprung back up. Everything was so quiet, the bushes with their little red flowers had turned into black lumps; it was impossible to imagine that by shining a flashlight we would see flowers.

I was thinking about the end of the world and Juliana and my tits when I heard the guitar chords, a strumming in stereo that filled the courts and the darkness, live and in Dolby directly from the Bible to the parking lot and to me, something or other announcing something from heaven, that something was over, that something was happening. I thought about Juliana and said, Jericho, aloud, and although no one was listening, I knelt. Then I realized what I was hearing was the start of the unplugged version of "Hotel California" coming from a car just a few meters from me. I got up and wiped the gravel and sand from my knees and approached the car and there, inside, was the swimming instructor, with a friend, the radio blasting, the two of them squeezing blackheads on each other's faces.

The friend was also an instructor, but of Spanish dances. Her name was Carmela and I knew her well cuz she supervised the lunch crew. I had my turn on Tuesdays. We all had to do it at least once. You'd stand behind the serving table and they'd give you a big serving spoon. When you weren't dishing out rice, you were serving hamburgers and hot dogs. I almost always had to serve sausages; I pinched them with a fork and put them on each plate. I did that for an hour until everyone was served. The best job is to serve drinks cuz while you're filling the glasses with ice or passing the Coke or Red Rock bottles you can drink one or two glasses yourself while standing there. The worst job is when they serve picapollo cuz it seems like they order it the day before and the chicken gets real cold, like a corpse, and the fried green plantains turn into greasy stones. It all stinks.

Sometimes they even give us dessert: flan or majarete that looks like shit. Sometimes it's tres leches, but it looks like barf.

One day I had to serve the drinks and I opened a Mirinda bottle for myself and when I poured it into a glass, there was a dead violet-colored lizard. I just stared at that sad sight strewn over the ice, as sad as a curse word. I showed it to the instructor, the swimming instructor's friend, and she made us check all the bottles. We found five containing creatures. Almost all were in Mirinda bottles. Cockroaches, lizards, earthworms: a collection worthy of a biology lab. At least there weren't fingers from people with AIDS.

The next day they served picapollo and a really foul odor ran through the whole camp cafeteria, which was actually the club's party room arranged with seventeen tables, one for each section, each with its own chairs and tablecloths. I was swallowing a green plantain I'd dipped in Coke to soften it when Rebeca had another epileptic fit and accidentally spilled the bottle all over the table.

Juliana, who was next to her, raised her hands to her head and said, That's bad, that's real bad luck, and threw salt over her left shoulder while Rebeca swallowed her tongue.

The instructors from the other sections came running to get salt, to throw salt over their own shoulders, and there was so much salt they had to call over the loudspeakers, asking all the campers to cooperate, but the more salt they threw over their shoulders, the more salt there was, covering their shoes, their knees, their shoulders. Luckily, I'd really improved my freestyle and was able to swim to the top of the gazebo's white ceiling. I climbed and waited for somebody to do something.

Everywhere, the white sea. An incredible thirst and not even a drop of Mirinda, though no one cares one whit, or one lizard. In the distance you could see the other gazebos' white tops and some kids who had managed to swim to one were preparing a campfire so they could cook Rebeca. When dusk came, the salt was whiter than ever and the sky was so orange it looked like it was gonna rain mandarin oranges. And just like every afternoon, Mami showed up wearing her sunglasses and her gray linen uniform from the savings and loan, driving her Nissan Sunny (which she's still paying for) over the salt as if it was a street. She gets out of the car, her gray silhouette progressing over the orange citrus, as if there was still a pool or a camp or anything. Without bothering to take off her sunglasses, she informs me that Papi has just been killed.

I see a car, a helluva car, a car, with its bumper and drivers. It smashes into him, it smashed him, it hasn't smashed him yet. Like a yellow orange like the juice of a yellow orange. A car hit him and squished him as if he were a yellow orange. Yellow oranges are for practice. Juggling, sick bay. In fact, they're oranges but they call them yellow oranges and they're juicy and yellow. They squeeze the seed out of you. The car comes and cuts him in half. He is, they are, two better halves. The first car, crazy. It crashed into you, it crashed into you. A driverless car, a headless driver. Here it comes. From the side, from behind, from straight ahead, from below as if the street were made of glass. The car, a helluva car. A car car car car, the most helluva car, car, attacking, attack it, fuck it, *chúbalo, chúbalo, chúbalo.* Car, car. He was killed over a car, over a car, a helluva an expensive car, so expensive. The cheapest expensive cars, expensive cars being too rare, one two, three cars pass and don't collide, but the fourth one sideswipes him, hits him on the side, batters him, and then there's another car, another car, another car running him over, but it's a recording of a car, and it's always the same car, looking the exact same. A car is a car. A car is a car is a car is a car, rolling over you, grinding into your face, running over you, just imagine how your eyes pop out. The grease stains in the shape of. Running right over you. Grinding into you. Breaking your bones. Your bones breaking. You've crashed, crashed. You, like a peel, like a garlic clove, car, car, there are smart cars, shrewd cars, cars in which people live. Caravans. Stains in the shape of. To the right, to the left, over the hip. He falls. He doesn't break. His guts explode. A car can kill you. A car takes off. A car car. That one, that one right now, the same one right now. The same car. Here it comes. Speeding up. Speeding up. Speeding up. It's a car, nothing else. It's not a car. It hit him again, and now we see the giant muffler blowing dark smoke on the dead body. Car, car, the car hurling death, dead car. Ghost car. Ghost ship. Some cars are ships. Like Chevrolets in the seventies, Impalas. A titanic car sinks into your paunch, a car sinks into your belly, they shove it up your ass. Well greased. From behind and up the front, everywhere. A brandless car, the most expensive car. What an expensive car. That car is too expensive. I want my car. My car. My car. Here it comes, turning the corner. Hold on, it's coming. Here comes the car. It hits you, it hits you, it deviates your septum, they operate, they replace your nose with a cashew. They sew up a car for you, they mechanize your liver with a Stillson wrench. A sharp car, a car gunning all over the place, with steel tires, like Ben-Hur's enemy. You don't have a license. You only have fifty pesos for the cops. For traffic. A body, a speed bump. They pay you. A corpse his car, the prey his car. I give you my car wash, I give it to you. Here it comes, here it comes again, now, right now, look at how it jumps, look how the car, look at how, look at how it falls. You can't see how it falls. It's still there. They stop him on a residential street, they clean off the blood with a sponge, a rag, a towel. With a little cotton ball with acetone. They clean the bumper with ethyl alcohol. With gasoline. Your champagne-colored car is not yours. It belongs to the dead, the prey, your car is not yours, none of them were his. The cars belong to the dead, the cars are going to heaven, the expensive ones never go to heaven. They're too heavy, they stay here. They're fucked. Who wants one, who wants a car, car. And a one. Erre con erre. And a three. Erre con erre. Fast fast. Over the top, over the top, where I told you before, the broken bones are so noisy, so noisy, so much noise. What do I owe you, driver, what do I owe you, I have to get off cuz they're gonna pass me, they're gonna run right over me, they're telling me I have to get out cuz it's my turn to get run over, the tires on the side, up the front, a million miles an hour, the muffler, in, like a tunnel. Now we see the underside of the car as if the street was made of glass. Of course. Here it comes, such dominance, the muffler sparking on all the speed bumps cuz there's a dead body in the trunk and the trunk weighs too much and the car is too low, right? Right, car? You're too too low? Right car, car car, little car, Carrie. The bloody car, the prophet car, the sleeping driver grinding the tires, spitting smoke. The driver is unseen. The headless driver. The car is approaching. And now and now, and now the car, the car, the car, comes back, around the corner, around the same corner, with the lights off, it's daytime, of course, and it hits him, hits him. Smashes him. Blows his guts. You see him like a doll flying through the air. It's a crash test dummy. It's Papi, it's a crash test dummy. It's Papi. It's a crash test dummy, and it hits him, hits him and throws him up in the air, it's a crash test dummy, coming this way, turning the corner and crashing right into him, so he doesn't get up, and crashes and disappears right into him, it's a tunnel, it's Papi, it's a crash test dummy, of course. The lights come on, it's dark, of course, from behind, it's an asshole, it's a tunnel, it's the car's muffler, car. Something strange comes in reverse. If you drive in reverse you can hear the devil. If you go in reverse you see me. Car, car, and the car comes back from the same corner, turns, the corner, the post and the light, the car passes by, the corner, the car turns again, the wheel turns, the driver's unseen. It's a crash test dummy, it's Papi, it's a headless driver. The bumper, the hood, the bumper, the hood. The body lies towards the top of the car and lands on the antenna. The antenna spears an eye. The eye explodes. The body doesn't fall. The body flies. The car flies, it's a crash test dummy. The car flies over the cemetery and wakes all the crash test dummies and Papi, and then the crash test dummies.

eleven

They're shoving a pill in my mouth. It's Mami. She has a little amber jar in her hand and she's kneeling next to my bed and plucking blue pills out of it and shoving them in my mouth. When I open my eyes, she says, Swallow, and gives me a glass of chocolate milk. I swallow and get up cuz the taste of metal on my tongue won't let me go back to sleep. I go to the bathroom and brush my teeth, to the kitchen where I love the way the sun filters in through Mami's balcony. I empty some Count Chocula into a bowl. I love Count Chocula. I love the marshmallow bats. But what I love most is the way the cereal colors the milk brown. If it's Franken-Berry then it turns the milk pink. I like that too.

When I open my eyes again, my mouth is full of Count Chocula and milk and I'm drooling. I'm naked and sitting at the dining room table while the sun continues to filter in through the balcony. Mami scrubs my arm with a sponge and reminds me: They called this morning; they killed your father.

I can't see my mom's face, it's just a pink blur, like milk

colored by those little marshmallow ghosts in Count Chocula, Franken Berry, and Boo-Berry. I cry and I don't even know why. Oh, cuz your dad died, that's why, the stain reminded me every time I opened my eyes. It was a marshmallow stain, and it said, They shot him in the head. And then the marshmallow would cry too.

The marshmallows carried me to my mom's bed cuz I couldn't even walk. You need mourning clothes, they said, and then they brought me a black Ocean Pacific T-shirt, but it had an orange and red landscape on the back, a Hawaiian beach. They tried to put it on me but my arms were as slippery as water, as loose as Muppet arms and I was worried the T-shirt would get marshmallow all over it. Somebody else was putting pants and shoes on me. I could hear myself starting to cry and I asked myself why and Mami, who was sitting at her dresser and putting on her pantyhose, would get up and run towards me with the pantyhose only halfway up her legs, the amber jar in her hand, and throw three more blue pills in my mouth.

They taste like crap.

When I finally got it together and was able to get up, we went to the beauty salon. Your dad doesn't like scarecrows, Mami tells me, but there was already a tear in her eye as she fumbled around in her purse for the little jar and took a pill with a chug from a bottle. Before we even went in the beauty salon, Mami said, Don't make a scene. So I swallow the last bits of pill clinging to one of my molars and enter the AC and the smells of hair spray and shampoo and burnt hair give me strength. Dominga, the salon owner, a fat woman with gold teeth and trucker hands and an enormous butt that looks like a marshmallow under that blue uniform, took me first. She declared she would take care of each of Papi's daughters without charging a fee and without appointment. A couple of girls with hair straighteners in their hands just got up and left. Women in wet smocks were coming left and right to get their highlights and dye and wax jobs. I was under the hair dryer and when I opened my eyes again Mami was with another stylist while she was getting her toenails done, surely talking about life and the drug trade. She chose a color for her toenails, lifting each little bottle from a tray and placing it next to her hand to compare her skin color and the polish.

When I opened my eyes again, we were on the highway and Mami was driving very slowly behind a giant truck. Its plates said 1952–789 and it was red. The truck was loaded with cassava and there were Haitians sitting in back, on the very edges of the truck, one wearing a red cap and the other, who was shirtless, holding on with one hand and using the other to keep himself from the cold, but he couldn't.

Mami opened the glove compartment and two or three things fell to the floor between my feet. One at a time. The first was a mini-vacuum that Mami never uses to clean the car seats. The other two were a rotten banana and newsletter number twenty-five from Carola de Goya's collection of esoteric notebooks, the edition in which she personally and directly translated Maestro Damlo Vetranbashe Praputi, who counseled from the fourteenth dimension how celestial armies should be utilized when it came time to dispatch a disembodied soul to seventh heaven or beyond.

Mami had used a yellow highlighter to mark the lines she wanted me to read aloud, which she had specifically requested. I read her Carola's instructions inspired by Vetranbashe himself, who suggested the following:

When the coffin comes into the enclosure, the initiate should stand close to it, but not too close, looking east and repeating:
Cut and undo, cut and undo, cut and undo, cut and undo.
Repeat while visualizing a blue light and a court of blue angels descending and arranging themselves around the coffin, using the blue swords in their fists to cut the ties (also blue) that join the coffin to the bodies of those present. In order to do this, first, we must visualize those present and the blue ribbons like umbilical cords that tie the coffin to those present. Those present are those in attendance at that moment, not everyone in this world, many are invisible and ethereal, which the initiate, no longer living, should visualize.

When I open my eyes again we are already in Papi's hometown. I recognize it cuz there's a World War II plane at the entrance with a shark's mouth painted on it. We stopped at a convenience store to buy crackers. Mami got out and when she game back she took off her sunglasses for the first time. What is the name of that illness that gives people black circles like charcoal under their eyes? Well, Mami had that.

I turn on the radio and I hear my tía Leysi with a chorus in the background screaming:
Oh they killed him, oh they killed him.
Oh my brother, oh they killed him.
Oh kill me.
They're so evil, they're so evil.
They shot him.

Mami changes the station with the same hand with which she's holding the little jar but China's screaming on the next station:

Guay, guay, guay, guay, guay, guay, take me with you, take me with you.

Mami's so frenetic when she changes the station that the little jar of pills falls and she stops the car next to the ditch and starts swallowing the pills that fell on the floor and tells me it's so they won't go to waste. And then, on another station, Cilí says:

My son, goddammit, my son, three bullets like the three nails that went into Christ.

When she's finished the DJ says I'll be there soon, live and in person, and in the background you can still hear the *guay guay*.

Mami can't take it anymore. She throws the empty jar out the window and crashes the car at the bottom of the ditch, which is dry cuz it hasn't rained in a long time. People are sitting outside their homes along the old highway and I don't know if they're waiting for rain or the funeral march.

When we get to the house in which Papi was born, it's already been turned into a museum. Mami makes her way through the line of tourists holding little balloons with Papi's portrait on them. When we're finally in front of the ticket office, Mami knocks hard on the glass, drooling, her lids as heavy as mine, which feel like stone. Mami grabs me, cuz my legs are no longer responding, and we make our way to the house, which is already full of Japanese blonds taking photos next to the golden potty that Papi supposedly used as a boy. I know this is not the house where Papi was born, cuz Papi was born in a house with a dirt floor.

Mami lets herself fall on the marble floor, and placing her head on a tourist's loafer as if it were a pillow, she asks, Where is Milly, where is Leysi, where is everybody?

When I open my eyes again, an old man is jostling me, a very tall man, dark skinned with very white hair and wearing a museum guard uniform with a name tag that says Pérez on his chest. He throws Mami over his shoulder and pulls me by the hand as we run towards a jeep. He explains: I'm your tío Fonso, I'm Fonso. Your abuela Cilí's brother. The funeral isn't here; this museum thing is to raise funds to pay for the funeral. We drive for a while on a side street with cracked red dirt, the red poinciana branches like match heads above the roof of the jeep. Fonso explains: We're going to the little house where your father was born, the little house with the dirt floor.

From afar we see a mob of people, a grill, and a cloud of smoke. But there's no little house. Leafy branches rise like buildings and the sun's rays cut through them to the smoke, like in a cigarette ad. There are groups of people sitting under trees, standing around drinking coffee, peasants with their donkeys and mules and bunches of green plantains like in a rum ad. The musicians from the local perico ripiao hold their instruments in silence while a group of paleros bring their offerings and are in turn offered a pair of chairs by a neighbor. Several women serve coffee in trays, each cup from a different china set. There are wooden chairs, plastic chairs, metal chairs here and there on the grass. Rocking chairs. A man burns cashew nuts and gives them to a group of kids. People look at me but they go on with what they were doing.

There's a pile of rocks under a mango tree, the only thing left of the little house where Cilí had her kids. Cilí, who's not crying, is sitting in a chair made of balsa wood, dressed in black and lilac, her hands on her knees. China and Leysi stand on either side of Cilí, hitting their chests with such force that with each blow little drops of blood fall from their eyes like lemon juice on anyone who comes near.

They're waiting for the body, Fonso tells me. The mothers of Papi's children make a circle around the little pile of rocks and extend their hands to touch Cilí, to console her, but Cilí doesn't even look at them, she doesn't do anything so the mothers say, in very loud voices, what a strong woman. Their children are dressed in mourning clothes.

When Cilí opens her eyes she see me and spreads her arms and I run towards her through the crowd that recognizes me now and wants to touch me and hug me while crying, and crying out, Little orphan girl, little orphan girl. Fonso protects me from the mob using Mami's body as a shield. She is still asleep and when we finally reach Cilí, Fonso puts Mami on the floor and I put her sunglasses back on. Cilí hugs me and says, My tears are dry. And then one, two, three, four or five buses from Onatrate arrive with more people and Fonso commands: More coffee.

People started burning up around one, when the sun was scorching and shone a blinding light on everything white, on every metal surface, and even on the black rags. You had to cover up with something. Go under the trees. The rays snuck through the leaves and pinched like a sulfur hail.

The crying continued but it was more of a humming commentary about the heat and the time and the dryness on everyone's lips. Somebody passed around some skin lotion cuz it was a cancerous sun. A live pig could be seen rooting in the distance and a couple of men were going crazy cuz they wanted to fry it up.

Cilí asked for water and some of the mothers of Papi's children ran to get it from a well about a hundred meters away but the water would evaporate in the glass on the return so they raced back. The well eventually went dry and they asked Fonso to go to the city and get a water tank.

It was a great shame. All this dry crying was a great shame and very noisy, so much so that Mami finally woke up, lifting her head from a rock, as confused as a cat, her hand going through her hair, surveying her surroundings with a look of satisfaction as if she'd just awoken in a five-star hotel. She checked the burned skin on her arms and said, Oh good, I got a little sun. Then she got up and realized where she was and started pushing little blue pills into her eyes. If she'd actually teared up, we would've drunk her tears. There was not a drop of rum left, or of coffee, or of anything, and Fonso was nowhere in sight. A troop of boy scouts left with a nun to see if they could find a river and they came back with two bags of white rocks so we could entertain ourselves painting faces on them with nail polish. The musicians wrung their shirts so they could drink their own sweat. The women fanned themselves until a dizzy spell caused them to tumble to the floor, one leg shaking.

At about four, we started to see extraterrestrials, diamonds, ovals, shiny dots in the blue sky that people would spot and point to with their fingers, about ten per second. They were made of silver. No—mercury, gold. They were flying saucers. They're here, they're here, said China, writing Welcome with coffee grounds on the ground. They've come for us, they've come for us, said Leysi, opening her arms and smiling with her lips sealed, writing Hallelujah on her eyelids. Cilí put her hand over her eyes to shield them and bit her lower lip. That's when Fonso arrived and parked the minivan. He got out and scratched his head cuz there were so many people on their knees, with their arms raised, pointing and shading their eyes at the same time. He looked up and told me: Those are American planes, spraying the clouds so it'll rain.

The planes disappeared and small clouds began to gather in the middle of the sky, clouds that looked like camels, like Fred Flintstone, like a boat with oars. The bigger clouds looked like Miss Piggy and Bart Simpson, and one little cloud looked like a coffee maker at first and then like a Jet Ski and then like a house with a chimney and then I don't know what, cuz the sky got as white as Styrofoam and a breeze raised dust and dry leaves, a crash of thunder split our eardrums once, then twice, and then everybody was really on their knees, getting up and falling on their knees again, forgetting about the dead man, about the funeral, about Cilí, about everything. They opened their mouths to catch the first drops. And some did.

Now we were all looking at the white screen of the sky, waiting for the rain as if it were the movie of our lives. And again: that sound like the opening and closing of steel gates that precedes lightning, and then the great cloud finally released its load. A cobalt-blue container with a parachute descended through the air and raised a cloud of dust when it finally landed. There was not a single cloud left in the sky, not one.

People started getting up and going towards it. Leysi opened her eyes with a half smile while Mami dried the pills as best she could so she could get a good look at the container, which now screeched and vibrated like an electric generator. One of the container's sides dropped and a ramp jutted out like a tongue. A kind of wheeled platform came down the ramp and rolled until it got to where Papi's birthplace had once been; there was a pearl-gray coffin on the platform. Mechanical arms popped out of a compartment and unfolded a tarpaulin, a great white tent that went over the coffin. There were five chairs, each with a name: Cilí, Leysi, China, Mami, and Me and a sign on each that said Reserved. Then a black woman who looked about forty years old came down from the container; she was wearing a T-shirt emblazoned with the name Etelvina and she pushed a cart with a thermos full of coffee and a stack of little paper cups. Behind her came two olive-skinned women dressed in black, their naps all matted, asking those present for the name of the deceased so they could start to wail. Behind them came the wreaths; one of the mothers of Papi's children took care to cover the banners with dedications. Then came the candles, the candelabras, and various business associates of Papi's who just looked at the ground and gave Cilí a pat on the shoulder, saying: I know, ma'am, I know. China got the nerve to go up to the coffin, tore the tag off one of the handles and read:

This package includes a dead body. A coffin. Various single and five candle candelabras. A box of candles. Five floral wreaths, all plastic so they will last. Silicone dew drops for the flowers are optional. Two wailers. Two coffee servers. One water fountain. The cadaver is guaranteed to rot in the next forty-eight hours. The cadaver will experience all of the states of decomposition once it leaves the packaging. Two shovels. One eulogy written by Gabriel García Márquez. There is no need for instructions, no need for an operator— simply lift the top and rest in peace.

China looks at the tag as if it's the calling card of a new friend named Rockefeller and, not realizing what she's doing, opens the box.

This is not him. This is his body. This is his body. They do the embalming in Miami. That is not my dad. You have to see, just look. You have to look at him. I don't wanna see him. That's not him. Just look, just look. That's his body. Touch him, yeah, touch it. That's just his body. Oh they killed him, oh they shot him. It's a robot. Thirty-six years old. He's rotting by remote control. It's his body, it's him. If your car is damaged, will I think it's you who's hurt? Oh take me with you. *Guay. Guay.* It's a robot. Close his eyes. Put a medal of the Virgin of Altagracia on him. It's a robot. Bring her over. No, I don't want to. Leave me alone, leave her alone. It's a robot. Look at him. Bring her over. Oh they killed him. Careful with her hair cuz she's pulling it. Tie her down, don't let her undress. She has to look. Open her eyes. It's a robot, it's a robot. It's his body. Yes, but just the body. It's a robot. It smells already. Science is so advanced. Bring some bayrum. It's a robot. He's alive. His eyelid moved. He smells. Close the coffin. Dissolve it in water. Close his eyes. Tell it to science. It's a robot, it's a robot. It's my dad, it's a pig, it's a souvenir. Put on some more coffee. My mouth tastes like shit. Stay at my house. That's your dad, see, give him a kiss. Who is breathing. S'okay. It's a doll. Swallow it. Don't bury him, he's not dead. It's a robot. It's a Christmas gift. Cuz he was an asshole, cuz he was handsome. Touch him, yeah, make her touch him. It's a robot, it's sleeping. Oh they killed him.

Oh little girl, now you got no dad.

The funeral continues. The women pull their hair out. When they don't have any left on their heads, they start in on their coochies. The kids draw doodles with charcoal on the ground and play with a piece of wet newspaper. The men serve the coffee cuz the women are busy tearing their hair out. At night we sleep right there, under the stars, and they close the coffin so the body won't get wet from the dew. Everyone gets cozy in their cars, on the buses, or walking fifty paces one way, then back, their arms wrapped around themselves.

I don't sleep, I stay awake, I sit on a tree trunk and swat the fruit flies until someone comes up and talks to me about Papi. I light my way in the dark with a lighter so I won't sit on an anthill. The only lights are the two-hundred-watt spots on the tent over the coffin. When nobody's looking, and when the watchman guarding the tent is busy under a guava tree with a girl, I go up to the coffin and open it. It's the perfect replica, almost. The reddened skin around the chin is exactly like Papi's, the nails and cuticles on his hands are impeccable. But I can't be fooled, this isn't Papi. I've told everybody's it a robot, but nobody believes me.

The manufacturers have taken care to add stitches to his forehead where the bullets supposedly entered. It's a masterpiece. Even I would have been fooled, if not for. This isn't Papi, it's not even his body. This isn't even a dead body. It's a robot. I touch it. Hard and dry. It's a robot. Nobody can fool me. No robot designed by Soviet Americans is gonna tell me . . . goddammit. It's a robot. It's a robot. I'm convinced. It's a robot. When I take a plastic fork I've been hiding since breakfast and stick it in the stitches on the forehead, there's no blood, only the smell of rust and rotten wood. It's a robot. Then I open an eye and I nail the fork in it. I open the mouth, and the smell of rust is the smell of a rusty garbage can. I open the mouth, I look inside. The manufacturers have taken care to copy his teeth, the cavities, the fillings, one by one. I know Papi has a false tooth and the robot knows too; I take it and look at it. I keep it. I put it in my pocket. Trumpets start to play, harps, Jericho.

Sirens, alarms protect the android. Guards with black helmets come out from under rocks, from Cilí's mouth, and Cilí herself comes at me with a machete in her mouth. Leysi, China, they all come at me with billy clubs to club me. They distributed Papi's golf clubs and baseball bats among themselves and now they're coming to beat me to a pulp. I run, I run and pull out the false tooth from my pocket and swallow it, I swallow it, I jump, I fall into a river, I swim, I splash about, I get out, I run, run, run, run, run.

It goes on like this for days, weeks, and years. Not so many years though. Really, it was just a few minutes. Maybe two or three. When I'm safely in the dark, squashing squashes with my feet, I stop. In the distance the voices of the black helmets and the tear gas are fading. It smells like gum. There's a smell of mint gum and Constanza cigarettes in the air. I look up and there's not a single star or light. The smell of mint gum and Constanza cigarettes blends with the cricket noise and fills my lungs. I squat and breathe, waiting for the blow that's gonna smash my skull like a pumpkin. I stay that way for hours or, well, whatever. Then there were lights up high, very white, and they blinded me cuz I had been years in the dark. They were headlights. On an old Mercedes from the seventies, from the eighties. Between the curtain of smoke from the Constanzas, the banana leaves, and the smell of mint gum, I recognized the Mercedes logo illuminated by its own light. And I knew I would be saved. Perhaps forever. I ran toward the light, squashing squashes with my feet, squashing the heads of the dead, and, well, I ran for years. When I was almost within reach of the Mercedes logo, I fell face first in front of the driver's-side door, which opened, and then there were one, two, patent-leather shoes with metal tips, fine hose, and under the Dubble Bubble mint smell, I detected the scent of Drakkar and looked up and saw the hair in silhouette, the wave, the wide and white smile like a waning crescent in that dark sky. It was Puchy, and then the other door opened and it was Milly. She was exactly the same, with her wave, her shoes, her waning crescent smile. Damn, what luck.

They say, *We came looking for you. You know better than them. Papi is not dead, Papi is alive. We were in New York and we saw him. We talked to him. He's there. He's waiting for us. He's coming. The day he comes back everybody's gonna be fucked, except us. We know better.*

We were in the Mercedes going very slowly down the side streets, the dry earth screeching beneath the tires. Puchy was explaining everything to me and he would pause now and then so he could run over some drunken peasant with a raised machete asking for my head. Their skulls would screech like dry earth. Puchy would look back in the rearview mirror and then go on: Papi knows too much. That's why he had to hide. His business associates wanna do away with him. His associates wanna keep Papi's stuff. They wanna rule the earth. They've made up Papi's death. Don't believe anybody, anybody. The associates have bought everybody out; some are descended directly from Atlas, from the Templars. Nanotechnology and BS; it's a conspiracy.

I feel very intelligent and now Milly and Puchy are talking at the same time and very fast, faster than the devil. Faster than the Mercedes. Sometimes they pause to run over a black hen crossing the road or to open and close the windows before and after Milly smokes a Constanza. Sometimes we stop at a roadside stand and Milly says, Two pasteles en hoja, and a lady shows up with the pasteles and charges us while drying her hands on an apron and the electric windows screech as they go up to close and the AC screeches as it cools my bones.

The twins are talking to me now with their mouths full of pastel and salsa picante and the salsa and the pasteles are also talking to me.

Everything will be different now, you'll see, say Puchy or Milly or the pasteles. And as soon as I heard that, I began to make sense of everything, as if a Rubik's Cube was falling into place in my head, and instead of color, yellow or red or blue, the pieces rotate and rotate and rotate and on each square there are people's faces, gestures, words, sunsets that begin to give shape to things while the rest move and move and on to infinity. In this way, Juliana was an envoy for the twins, and Soti was an archangel and the same for those little pastries I had that Easter Sunday. I saw rays shining and tying everything together. It was very clear. Papi was in me, and I was in Papi. I even licked the salsa picante from Papi's impeccable cuticles. I was exactly the same as Papi. I was Papi. I am Papi.

Later I fell asleep and everything was revealed. The place, the mission, the mysteries. I'd wake up from a little dream and would tell the twins where to turn. They were driving the Mercedes and would stop now and then to get gas and cheese sticks. We saw every landscape on the island: woods, desert, and coast, cuz the revelations had us all out of sorts. I was in the backseat, dreaming about our mission, waking up only to recite another short verse so Milly could write it down on a napkin. Whenever we weren't sure which way to go, Milly would sing me a song so I could go back to sleep, usually "Everybody Wants to Rule the World" by Tears for Fears. I'd fall asleep again and a very old man with a long white mane and beard, or a little blond boy with blue eyes, would show me maps on plasma screens, and sometimes they'd get mixed up, and instead of directions, they'd give me lottery numbers and I'd jot them down without telling the twins. It went on like this for years. Honest. Up and down. More revelations than the devil. So many, in fact, that Milly bought a cardboard accordion file folder to keep all the napkins, the scraps of paper, the receipts on the back of which she'd scribbled what I'd dictated.

Apart from the list of things we needed for the mission (tape recorders, photocopiers, toilet paper), I'd started a wish list for our team (a Walkman for Milly, a lifetime supply of cologne for Puchy, and Saona Island for me). It dawned on Puchy that we had to find a place, a kind of sacred space or something like that. So Milly sang me Rick Astley's "Together Forever" and, while I was falling asleep, I thought Milly had finally given up Tears for Fears. I dreamt Nat King Cole was singing: toma chocolate, paga lo que debes. When I woke up, I told the twins we had to stop to buy lottery tickets and I started spewing numbers. We spent all our money and that was the first miracle: not a single ticket won.

The following Sunday I convinced Puchy to sell the Mercedes so we could buy more lottery tickets. The Sunday after that we were going door to door begging and three Sundays after that we were so dirty and stinky from sleeping on the streets and dumpster diving that we looked like real prophets. We numbered forty when we entered San Juan de Maguana, where the San Juan Paleros (which were actually all the landowners, government employees, and ordinary people of San Juan) came out to welcome us in vans and jeeps cuz they were waiting for us and they guided us through the weeds, lighting the way with their halogen lamps until we arrived at the perfect place for the settlement, a clearing between the brambles, the rain trees, and the brush. As soon as we got there, Milly pulled out her gun and shot a wandering black goat which we ate with a side of chenchén. Everyone ate as we sat on the ground, licking their fingers, then they went into the forests to gather sticks or break off branches to make little houses or drums. By sunrise, they'd erected three houses using mud, wood, and hay, one to be used as a temple and the other two for lodging for the people. At about noon, two vendors came by. I healed the daughter of one and his bull calf too. I pulled forty-nine worms from the other guy's foot. At about six, the mayor and his wife showed up, bringing with them a little TV and a PlayStation console so I'd entertain myself and by evening, in an operation that lasted four hours, we had three lamp posts, a transformer, and enough wiring for bulbs and outlets.

I asked that the lights be turned off cuz the moon was so full and you could see the whites of everyone's eyes. A girl from the capital brought me a loudspeaker, along with a list of people who believed Papi was alive. She explained there was a website where people could see a photo of Papi, sign up, and make a request. Right there and then I made her chief of media and propaganda for Papi's next earthly administration. She dropped to the ground, overtaken by the spirit of Asela Mera or Zoila Luna, I'm not sure which. More people began to arrive in buses, minivans, mules, with flags, posters, and songs they'd come up with about Papi and about me:

We got the key
To join this race
A thousand white Mercedes
One for whomever keeps the pace

My Papi has great power
Look how strong and fast he is
Red is the color of his bat
And at softball he's a wiz

At eight in the morning I stood at the pulpit that had been built in front of the temple and read the new prayer. People cried and jiggled their raised key chains. Then more people came, grown-ups and kids and pets, with camping equipment and gifts for me: peanut butter, guava juice, German porn on VHS tapes, all so that when Papi returned, he'd do something for them, cure their toothaches and such. I had them calling for Papi after a quick slap. But what people liked most was to be called upon and so, from my inflatable chair with velvet wheels, I passed out titles left and right: delegate for Papi's telepathic circumcision, viceroy of Papi's state of siege, commander in chief of all of Papi's messes. I did it all to the rhythm of pre-pre-hip-hop, techno shootout and minimal merengue, which the paleros improvised along with some Norwegian DJs brought in for the occasion. The kilometer between our settlement and the nearest town was now lined with food stands and gift shops managed by Puchy where, for a modest price, you could buy key chains with replicas of Papi's dick, including his Mercedes-Benz logo tattoo, and CDs of my recorded voice so people could hear me listing more than a thousand different titles they could own, all guaranteed to take immediate effect upon Papi's next earthly administration.

One day, I think sometime in July, the apparitions started. People began to see Papi everywhere. In the parking lots, in the woods, near the drinking fountains, at a cheap diner on the outskirts of town. I thought people were going crazy. Every morning when people gathered in front of the pulpit to hear me, I would calm them down by explaining the new terms on which Papi's next earthly administration would make its triumphant arrival on the world scene: signs, black helicopters, extraterrestrials, earthquakes, sour milk, stinky cheeses, stale Doritos. Around that time, journalists showed up and took my photo as well as photos of the altar, which was in fact just a photo of Papi, a cup of Chivas Regal with seven upside-down daggers, and a gold cell phone. They wanted to interview me and ask me about the nine-year-old girls who were getting pregnant in the settlement and I said, It's just that Papi's power is overwhelming, it's all over the place.

By November people were getting desperate. Some were saying Papi even talked to them and I thought maybe we needed a psychiatrist to get group therapy going or something. Sometimes I'd be at the pulpit speaking and I'd see somebody throw themselves from a balcony, panic stricken, and screaming, I saw him, I saw him, before crashing to the ground. I told them what they were seeing were simply ethereal releases of ghostly molecules from the regulating specter of the cosmic memory of the great power that is Papi, and which manifested in moments of great expectation. Another day I told them the Papi they were all seeing was nothing more than the result of a plan by his business associates to confuse the believers, that it was an impostor, and that when Papi actually returned, he would do it like a king and everyone would see him. Another day I told them it was the Fifth Apostle of the cross of Caravaca, and yet another I said it was the Templars, then NATO, then Dr. Spock from *Star Trek*.

They hung garlic when I told them it was a vampire, drank castor oil when I said it was the result of pneumonia, and then one day, in the evening, when I was strolling and thinking about that new PlayStation that was on its way in the hands of some pilgrim, I got thirsty and walked over to the Coke machine behind the temple. The white and red halo illuminated the woods and I pushed in five coins and pressed the button, all the while appreciating the dry stalks and the new green buds on the trees. When the can didn't drop, I gave the machine a couple of swift kicks. I felt a sudden shiver and my throat completely dried up. Not a soul was awake and I wanted to run cuz I'm always scared of places with vending machines. I kicked the machine again and it purred. I squatted to see if it had returned my change but there was nothing. That's when he appeared before me, barefoot, right next to the machine, wearing the same suit in which they had buried him, a little medal of the Virgin of Altagracia pinned to his jacket, the buttonhole crooked. He smelled and looked as bruised as a zombie. He opened his mouth and pointed to his false tooth, or rather, the space where the tooth should have been, the tooth I had extracted and swallowed before fleeing his funeral. I shitted out that tooth a long time ago, Papi, I heard myself tell him, and he closed his mouth, which had been emitting a fartlike odor. The Coke can finally dropped and I grabbed it. The dead robot could not speak very well. He could ask for water but since he was in the process of decomposition it was best not to give it to him cuz the stink would just get stronger. The rotting was guaranteed by the manufacturers and I felt bad for him, wandering aimlessly like an apparition that didn't understand he would soon be transformed into fertilizer.

I called a meeting. Puchy sprayed the air with gardenia and asked me if I was sure. First, I thought I would just tell the crowd the truth: What you've seen isn't Papi, it's not a zombie, it's nothing. It's a body, an android cadaver sponsored by Opus Dei and the Colombian mafia that was used during Papi's so-called official funeral, but the robot has a manufacturing defect and left the grave instead of laying still and rotting. But instead, so as not to scare them, I said, Here's Saint Lazarus, raised from the dead through Papi's great power in me. Thus the stink. We put a fake beard on him so people wouldn't suspect, and some green Capri pants, but we left him shirtless so people could see the sores and the multicolored worms. The people said, A miracle, a miracle, and plucked the worms off him to make bronze replicas and then put the bronze worms on Papi's altar. Since he didn't make pronouncements as he rotted, nor perform miracles, but rather just stared at the horizon for long periods with his robot eyes, his resolute dead man's eyes, people became convinced he was a chosen one.

One day he started coming apart from the inside and a bit of his intestines poked out of his lower belly. I continued to be very impressed by the advances in science that took such details into account. He got used to the settlement and was soon integrated into all the rituals, especially after Puchy found him writing graffiti on a wall with a turd and we bought him Magic Markers and sprays and paints so he could develop his talent. The people just loved his drawings and began to say Papi guided his hand, that it was Papi's own hand that traced those symbols. Groups formed to interpret the stinky saint's graffiti; they met on Thursdays, they had their own chat room.

We became famous and would appear in the media now and again, accused of reviving the cult of Papi, of superstition, of prostitution, of rape, of deflowering virgins, of taking children out of school, of chewing gum, of destroying the national economy, of not accepting food from the Peace Corps, of prohibiting our followers from voting, of telling them to vote, of giving refuge to Trujillo supporters, to communists, to deserters, of distributing firearms, of actually being Haitians, of trafficking in sacred objects belonging to Haitian voodoo, of eating dirt, of conspiring against the government, of conspiring against the cardinal, of sacrificing babies, of training our followers in kung fu and aikido and capoeira, of having a foul mouth, of being dirty, of extorting an ignorant population, of being ignorant, of murdering nuns, of fucking nuns, of dressing up as nuns, of dancing naked on the rooftop as nuns walked by, of being into the occult, of listening to Marilyn Manson, of listening to Tulile, of being drag queens, of being homophobic, of trafficking in the organs of elitists, artists, activists, magicians, charlatans, fascists, *Tarde Alegre* columnists, bohemian thugs, pedophiles, of reading Nietzsche, of being illiterate, of having Chinese or Arab parents. Of being terrorists.

Our photos would appear on the front page. Me with my PlayStation console, Puchy with his Lysol spray, and Milly and her Walkman. The caption would explain how terrorists use ordinary technology in their criminal acts against the world. There would be red circles on the photos marking my PlayStation console, the gardenia spray, and Milly's Walkman, respectively, as irrefutable proof of nuclear arms being used by remote control, of biological weapons in their final phase, and the sophisticated tele-communication network operating from our base. And then the biggest photo of all, the photo of the shirtless dead robot with his nylon beard sitting on a cinder block, surrounded, the people's gaze following the little twig in his saintly hand as he scribbled his earthly graffiti. The caption identifies him as "the brains of the operation," "the real blood sucker," the guerrilla trained in Albania by the descendants of Fu Manchu. Next to the photo there were two or three graphics along with his drawings, which look like digital circuits, and maps of the island super-imposed on them which proved the lines were nothing but plans for attack, or rather, "access maps to the under-ground tunnel system where the reptilian brethren and Neo-Nazi mutants, whose collaboration with the sect is well known, live."

Then it's Papi's birthday and for a whole week there are trucks coming in, trucks with chairs, tents, stands, lights, stages, sound systems, and thousands of tons of fire-works for the spectacular conclusion. More people come, and then even more come in trucks, buses, small planes that drop them without parachutes on the platform just to get things going. There are still a few technical details to deal with and in the meantime we put on a Maná CD for four hours worth of entertainment. They applaud, they come up with slogans, they improvise music with empty Snapple bottles. When least expected, there's a stuttering electronic boom and the people run to the platform and I come out. The people are in a bad way, they shout, they scream, they shake. Some young girls faint and the people lift them up and float them over to the stage on a sea of hands. The security people take over. I say, one, one, two, can you hear me? The people are in a bad way, they shout, they scream, they shake. Some young girls faint and the people lift them up and float them over to the stage on a sea of hands. The security people take over. I finally begin: Papi is like Jason. Applause, hallelujahs, amens. He shows up when you least expect him. Applause, hallelujahs, amens. But what makes Papi most like Jason— applause, hallelujahs, amens—is that he always comes back, even when they kill him off. The people are in a bad way, they shout, they scream, they shake. Some young girls faint and the people lift them up and float them over to the stage on a sea of hands. The security people take over. My Papi has more of everything than yours. The people get up, dance in circles, say, Praise be to him who is holy. My Papi has more cars than the devil. Hallelujah, hallelujah. Ovation.

The program transpires exactly as announced on the event poster: music, prophecies and the end of the world, in that precise order. Three hours later (when the end had been planned), there were seven hundred thousand souls raising their arms and waiting for Papi to take them, and Papi was still talking through my mouth: Here I come. We heard a voice that came from the heavens, saying, Surrender now, there's still time. The people knelt, some protecting their heads with their bottles of Gatorade. I saw how the white helmets emerged from the forest and suddenly there was a shootout and the believers fell into piles. People were confused, some believing this was Papi, so they ran toward the helmets with open arms, especially cuz they were white. The white helmets did away with anything that moved and then they destroyed the platform, the houses, demolished the buildings and filled the pools with dirt and cement. Everything happened in about two hours. They went into the woods and chased down those who were still alive and had managed to escape. They put guns to their necks and made them dig a mass grave and pick up the Styrofoam cups and the plastic bottles left over from the concert, and then pick up the dead and bury them. When the press finally arrived, all they could do was take pictures of a bloody shoe that had been left behind in the commotion, a lost boy who was bawling his head off, and Lázaro's body, which the guards had been ordered to leave unburied so people would learn a lesson. He remained on that table, bearded and barefoot, according to the newspaper caption, just like the warring rebel they'd taught to fight during his training in the Sierra Maestra. The photo captured a rebel who had survived three hundred sixty-eight battles before defeat and still had the look of life in his eyes; that photo went around the world and very soon the bookstores were full of biographies and memoirs written by alleged lovers and classmates. There were T-shirts and posters and lollipops with that photo.

The survivors, one hundred forty-four total, were all jailed in a colonial prison, and day and night loudspeakers would preach about the reign of the father, the imminent coming of our lord, encouraging us to give up the backward African practices of our settlement and to accept the good news from the hands of a priest who came down every day to lead a mass and read the Bible to see if someone would confess something. If they didn't respond by confessing, they took them up, one by one, to the second floor where two hairy-bellied sergeants would tickle them, would pull out their fingernails, shove hungry rats up their asses, etc., etc. Everyone confessed. They said I was Papi's daughter, that the twins were my cousins, and that the bearded guy was nothing more than an android. When everyone passed the lie-detector test, they sent them to an insane asylum, where they found no priests, no torturers, but plenty of anthropologists.

twelve

She showed me her ball. It was in a glass jar that still had a Maggi mayonnaise label; it was on her nightstand next to a floral arrangement, and just like she'd said, it was about the size of a softball. They had to take everything out, they hollowed me out, Mami told me as she lifted the sheet so I could see the centipede-like scar from which a flesh colored tube drained into a see-through bag resting next to her bed and filled with urine and blood.

I would arrange her pillows and give her back rubs cuz it's painful to lie down for such a long time. I also gave her foot rubs and head rubs and told her jokes so she would laugh and plead with me not to make her laugh cuz it hurt. Then I would arrange her pillows again and raise or lower the bed by turning the handle. The room was dark and whenever we failed to turn on the lamp I would stub my toes against the edge of the bed and the other furniture and she would tell me to put my shoes on, that I would get sick from walking on that floor. I would lay down on the couch next to the bed, which was the longest couch I'd ever seen, upholstered in a wine-colored vinyl, and I would cover up and listen to her breath coming and going, coming and going, and sometimes I would even count her breaths as if I were one of those little machines they place next to sick people that go *tick tick tick tick*.

Sometimes she'd ask for the remote control and turn on the *Cristina* show. Today's guest was Luis Miguel, who Mami likes so much, but Patrick Swayze is who Mami likes most, especially after she saw Ghost; she says Whoopi Goldberg is really funny. Whenever Mami says someone is really funny I think it must be something bad, though she does laugh a lot with Whoopi Goldberg and everything, but when she says someone is really funny there's something inside Mami that's saying something else.

Sometimes people come to see her and they bring her passion-fruit ice cream, but it would always go bad cuz the mini-fridge in the room doesn't get cold enough. Sometimes they'd bring chocolates and she'd say, You eat them, it'll make me happy, and I'd eat them to make her happy. Sometimes she'd get a craving for a Coke cuz she had gas and I'd walk down to the clinic basement, which terrified me, but it's where the vending machines are, saying aloud: Please don't appear to me, please don't appear to me. When I got to where the vending machines were and dropped in the coins, I'd keep my eyes on the black hole where the can of Coke would land and not look anywhere else, sure that if I looked behind me I'd see a dead body.

When I returned to Mami's room she'd ask me if everything was going okay at school and I would say yes. I'd stay with her for many days and ask her if she needed anything and then run to the cafeteria across the street to buy a pork sandwich which I'd sneak past the nurses at the nursing station under my T-shirt cuz hospital food is so bad. Almost always soups. I'd go to school and then back to her room. My friends were almost all children of other patients and they all left very soon, although some came back to visit and we'd meet in the clinic hallway to smoke and exchange little packets of *Condorito* and Game Boy games, never stepping too far from the rooms in case our mothers needed us.

Mami's ball grew in silence. She didn't even notice. For a long time she thought it was sciatica cuz her leg would fall asleep and hurt, stuff like that. But everything happened cuz the ball was putting pressure on a nerve, attached as it was to the uterus and her ovaries and, even before cutting it out, the doctor told her it was the size of a softball.

I imagined a ball with stitches, a dirty white ball inside my mother, and also how, once it was taken out, we'd play with it and I would hit it out of the park with a bat like Sammy Sosa.

When Mami was ready to leave the clinic they found another ball, this one the size of a golf ball; it was on her breast, a benign tumor, of course. She sent me to my abuela's house cuz hanging out at the hospital was not doing me any good. I was at my abuela's house for several years and I'd receive letters from my mother with photos of her balls (tennis, badminton) and I'd put them up on the bathroom mirror, inserted between the mirror and the frame. I'd ask myself why cysts were round and not triangular or cubed and when we went back to school and the teacher asked us to write a composition about what we had done during our vacation, I wrote one entitled "My Mother's Balls," and I got an A−.

I went to see her one afternoon and found her crying and I didn't know what to do. She said two of Papi's business associates had been by and told her Papi owed them a lot of money, and they knew Papi had taken life insurance out on me and they thought it was only natural we should assume Papi's debts, and that there were many ways to pay that debt and the best was to pay them with the life insurance. The whole time they kept showing Mami pictures of their kids that they kept in their wallets.

I knew those business associates from when Papi was alive and I'd visit at the dealership. They talked all the time about wanting to club somebody in the balls. I moved back to the clinic and now, since we couldn't sleep, Mami and I would entertain ourselves by playing memory games. For example, we'd try to remember somebody's name. Mami would describe him physically and I would say, Yes, yes, that guy, and then we would begin listing names that began with the letter A (Arturo, Alejandro, etc.) and we'd go through the whole alphabet until we'd come on the name. Sometimes we'd list surnames instead of names, or women's names when we were trying to remember a man's name, which was very funny. In the end, it was always her who remembered and when we got to H and I said Homero, or Hans, she'd say: Hilda Saldaña, Hilda Saldaña, and I wouldn't even know who that was so I never would have remembered.

When Christmas came, Mami told me to spend more time at Cilí's house so I could drink golden cream punch and make sunglasses from bread crusts. I'd go to Cilí's and come back with grapes and treats rolled in sugar, all wrapped in a napkin. She'd say Santa Claus was coming and ask me what I wanted even though it'd been a long time since I believed in Santa Claus and she knew it. On TV we'd see the president at the door of his house, distributing gifts, scenes from the previous year in which women and children would get in line at dawn so they could receive a doll, a jump rope or a bicycle. I think they give out a bicycle for every thousand dolls.

One day Cilí tells me, Let's go to the cathedral, and I say I wanna go see Mami and she says no, there's a concert by the national choir. So we go to the cathedral and there's a mob, and before the concert starts there's a commotion and then silence and it's that the president, Balaguer, has arrived. He's blind and people are quiet as he slowly shuffles his feet, one of his sisters at his side. They sit in the front pew, and for a moment I think if I could get close to Balaguer, and if I could put my hands on him, I could heal him and he'd be able to see. I don't know where this idea comes from and I don't tell anyone cuz they're gonna think I'm crazy.

When I go back to the clinic I open the door to Mami's room and find an empty bed without a wrinkle on the sheets. I get a pain in my chest but I just stand there at the half-open door without knowing which way to go cuz everybody knows a made bed in a hospital means some-one has died. But then I hear her, coming down the hall-way and being very chatty with the nurse who's helping her, and she's wearing her purple-flowered gown and her hair is stuck to her head from so much time on a pillow. Mami raises her hand to greet me and it's the same hand with which she's carrying her bag of urine and blood, and she smiles at me and I smile at her, and then she says: I can stand up now and even walk a little but I'm still gonna need your help to go to the bathroom.